by Battersea Bridge

JANET DAVEY

Chatto & Windus
LONDON

Published by Chatto & Windus 2012

2 4 6 8 10 9 7 5 3 1

First published in Great Britain in 2012 by
Chatto & Windus
Random House, 20 Vauxhall Bridge Road,
London SW1V 2SA

www.randomhouse.co.uk

Addresses for companies within The Random House Group Limited
can be found at:
www.randomhouse.co.uk/offices.htm

The Random House Group Limited Reg. No. 954009

A CIP catalogue record for this book
is available from the British Library

ISBN 9780701186920

The Random House Group Limited supports The Forest Stewardship Council
(FSC®), the leading international forest certification organisation. Our books carrying
the FSC label are printed on FSC® certified paper. FSC is the only forest certification
scheme endorsed by the leading environmental organisations, including Greenpeace.
Our paper procurement policy can be found at
www.randomhouse.co.uk/environment

Typeset in Sabon by Palimpsest Book Production Ltd,
Falkirk, Stirlingshire

Printed and bound by CPI Group
(UK) Ltd, Croydon, CR0 4YY

BY BATTERSEA BRIDGE

To Dee and Mary-Anne,
and in memory of Katharine

'If I should return during my absence, keep me here until I come back.'

Price's Textbook of the Practice of Medicine, 9th edition

Part One

1

The two Mostyn boys had inscrutable faces. Pale and oval with neat little mouths and firm jaws – like male Madonnas. When the telephone rang: 'Leave the room, Netticles. This will be a private conversation,' though, more often than not, retreating, Anita would hear the words, 'My mother is out.'

Everything was private. The word, as used, meant 'important', 'urgent'; it lost its quiet, secluded aspect.

Of her two brothers, Mark was the one whose love Anita most wanted. Barney, the firstborn, jollied Anita along and talked like a young, inexperienced uncle. Mark, the middle child, was aloof.

'Take her,' they used to call to whoever was in earshot, waving her away. All children do this to baby siblings. It only becomes a memory if it carries on. They also ran from her, in a staged way, arms flailing; across the passage or up the stairs – and slammed a door. They stood on the other side, ready to add their weight when Anita tried the door-knob.

Just occasionally, they gave her their full attention,

needing a minion for some play they were enacting. 'Wait there and when I say "Now," you must . . .' Eyes beamed down at her.

She was mystified, never quite grasping the game that she assumed had a preordained form but which turned out always to be devised on the hoof and to end in disappointment. There was a moment, though, at the beginning, when she was filled with hope; wild with an excitement which she reined in, in order to concentrate.

Brigitte, the most durable of the au pair girls, used to ask Mark and Barney to take their sister out, in return for cigarettes. Their preferred route was across the field, along the lane and into the less picturesque part of the village. They shot down an alley between the studio photographer and the vintage car-hire firm and climbed on to the railway embankment wall, hauling Anita up after them. Once over, they started to walk along the flat verge at the top of the slope. Trains tore by; fast as plasters ripped off to avoid pain. In the lulls, Anita saw the rails. They had a dull finish, even the live one. She wished that the electrified rail had a special glint so that she would know to avoid it when she lost her footing and rolled over and over down the slope.

'Come on, Netticles, this is the good bit,' the boys said when they reached the shingly section which slipped away sheer down the cutting.

'No,' Anita said.

'What's that?' Mark and Barney were already ahead and edging their way with slick, sideways steps.

'Wait,' she said – though they never did – and Anita went with her stomach pressed to the wall and her fingers digging into the mortar, as the gap between them widened.

Further along was a breach where the bricks had fallen down and then she was up and over every time and on to the concrete path where the public were allowed to go. Anita picked the chippings out of her palms, with Mark, out of sight, yelling, 'Here comes "The Scorcher".' There was nothing to look at on the path – the backs of garages, the graffiti tamely achieved at ground level. The chips of brick made red dents in her flesh which saddened Anita because she was little and still loved her own skin. She wanted to see the train that rushed to the West Country. She made promises to herself that the next time she would be brave but she knew the promises were papery. She couldn't help being there – on the pedestrian side of the divide. Whenever she came to the fallen-in bricks, her legs turned into machines for taking her to safety.

Anita grew up believing she was behind and would never catch up. Her brothers came top and won prizes. She accreted small-scale possessions to assemble a personality, though attempts at artistry were thwarted by their cleaner who arranged things in lines. Pheasant feathers, seaside pebbles, beads and bracelets, after a dusting, looked like crime exhibits.

In her brothers' absence, Anita would open their cupboards – the confusion of socks and underpants, school ties and jockstraps – and, if she were feeling especially abject, go downstairs to the yellow room and find the school reports in the bottom drawer of her mother's desk. There was no need to take them out of their elastic bands; simply by riffling through, allowing air to circulate, she could mesmerise herself with half-glimpsed alphas. Her own reports were on blue flimsies and kept somewhere different.

'She's not as . . .' Veronica began. But did her mother actually say that? The rest was a given; it would never have formed part of the sentence. Whether the words were spoken or unspoken, a sigh, accompanied by a frisson that began in Veronica's head and travelled down into her shoulders, like an electrical charge, finished the matter off.

Veronica's old school – which Anita should have gone to – was worthy, not as worthy as Howard's, obviously, but solid enough and dating back to the 1890s. Had Anita scraped together the requisite exam marks and donned the maroon blazer – a disaster with her hair colour – her mother might have looked on her more favourably. She would have reminded Veronica not of her own schoolgirl self but of the scatterbrained and deeply silly Jills and Elfridas who had frittered away opportunities all those years ago. Nevertheless, she would have reminded her of *something*. Unless Anita had been expelled – not an impossible outcome – a bond would have been forged.

Anita observed her brothers but it was the wrong kind of observation – sharpened by the pain of being left out and therefore overfocused. She missed things. Even when she stopped being a child, memories confused her perception; she was unable to run a clean piece of film. She was the odd one and the boys were united. She saw no space between them. Brotherly love was authentic. Girls fell out. Anita knew this from school and also from Veronica. Boys were 'less devious', 'more straightforward', 'easier'.

Anita took the comments on board, not thinking to ask where Veronica stood in it all. She was a mother. Had she mastered a rope trick and emerged unmarked, or simply been an exception, a kind of honorary boy, all along?

2

Anita was surprised to see Laurence Beament at the Affordable Art Fair, though he was the kind of person who cropped up. He put himself about, keeping tabs on any number of people who never thought about him. Seeing his head pop round the edge of the stand wasn't unforeseeable but it gave her a jolt. Her smothered squeak came out like a gasp of pleasure.

'Mossy.' Laurence beamed and lunged towards her.

She turned her face abruptly to the right. The kiss landed in the soft place between her left cheekbone and her chin, leaving a faint musty smell, like brine in a jar of old olives.

'What are you doing here, Laurence?' she said.

'Looking. Browsing.'

'Really? Battersea? I wouldn't have thought you came south of the river.'

'I *like* trade fairs. Walking up and down the aisles, chatting to the sales people. What are *you* doing here, Mossy?'

'Oh, I'm just manning a stand for a friend. He had to go to Brighton.'

'You look the part.'

'Affordable, you mean?'

Laurence snorted in an amiable way. 'What have you got?' he asked, his dull, bulbous eyes fixed on her.

Anita Mostyn was in her mid thirties, with a prettiness that she had recently complicated by overplucking her eyebrows and dyeing her hair vanilla blonde. She wore kaleidoscope colours – a pink T-shirt and a green cardigan with crystal buttons. The more sober black and white keffiyeh was tied as a skirt over skinny jeans.

Laurence, only a few years older, had settled into a jaunty middle-aged look: suit, leopard-print tie, coat with velvet trimmings. The crinkly, copper-coloured hair that had been a menace in his teens, he now combed back flat. It ended in a slight flick-up where it hit his collar and gave him an air of thuggishness.

Laurence had always hankered after Anita Mostyn. She had a naïve sweetness that appealed to him. He had better luck with vigorous but discordant women. They sparred with him, charged into sex, and sooner or later dissolved in tears. He noted the bright, abstracted expression on Mossy's face and wondered whether she was currently attached. She had never had anything to do with him except allow herself to be cornered on social occasions. The two of them weren't exactly alone now – the public wandered past – but the person selling contemporary Japanese prints opposite had for the moment disappeared. The booth on H aisle, like all the booths, was an intimate place within the vast tent. Temporary walls that separated one from another were little more than head height. The halogen lighting was focused and hot. Laurence took a large spotted handkerchief from his trouser pocket and dabbed his brow.

'Mossy?' he said, to remind her that he was there.

Anita waved her arms airily. 'A selection of seaside oils. Turquoise sea and white villas. They're ironic, I think. Or possibly not. And some small bronze monkeys.'

Laurence scanned the walls and the display table.

'This isn't your kind of thing, is it?' Anita asked.

'I don't know. It might be.' He picked up a monkey from the collection and sat it on the flat of his hand. The creature squatted by the base of his thumb, squinting up at him through glass eyes. Laurence wandered slowly round the tiny brightly lit compartment, balancing the monkey, his flapping coat better suited to the turning space of the Royal Academy.

'Dull,' he pronounced after a few stately circuits. 'Who's the gallery-owning friend?'

'Oh, Niels just helps out. He's not the owner of Holy Cow. He's a voice coach. It's all about breathing. Mine's total crap.' Anita touched her ribcage and took a few deep breaths to demonstrate.

Laurence watched, mystified.

'Are you going to buy that monkey?' Anita asked.

Laurence hooked the C-shape of the tail over his little finger and dangled the animal upside down. 'Do you think my godson might like him?'

'He might. How old is he?'

'Fifteen months. Johnny Southern's boy. What do you think?'

'Perfect, I should say.'

Laurence parted with two hundred and fifty pounds and Anita agreed to meet him in a restaurant near Battersea Bridge on the Chelsea side. His musty smell lingered in the booth for the remaining hour she was there.

3

Wriggling her way through the loud drinkers in the downstairs bar, Anita realised that this was the place to be – not a table for two on the upper floor. She smiled a fixed smile as she shoved, and men with loosened ties allowed her a path through. If, by chance, she were the first to arrive she would call Laurence and suggest the bar. The comforting, raucous noise followed her up the stairs.

She hesitated in front of the restaurant door – began to count the brass upholstery nails that secured the padded velvet panels. She adjusted the black and white scarf, undoing the knot at her hip, unwinding and rewinding it. Only when the cloth gripped like a corset did she refasten it and push the door. As it closed behind her, deadening all sound, she saw Laurence at the far end of the lamplit room. He was sitting on a banquette with his back to the wall. A spindly, silver ballroom chair waited for her on the other side of the table. The champagne glass in front of Laurence was half empty. He had the look of someone settled. The question of his turning up after her had never arisen.

A waiter approached and helped Anita out of her coat. She walked down the room, past empty tables.

Laurence looked up when she pulled out the chair. 'Ah, Mossy,' he said.

She slid cautiously down. Laurence stared at her head. He seemed just to have noticed the extraordinary thing she had done to her hair; the bleached spikes, too pale for her face, that sprouted from her scalp. He ran a hand over his own head. 'The hair. It suits you.'

'Oh Larry, do you think so? It didn't turn out as expected.'

A waiter unwrapped the champagne from its napkin and filled her glass.

'How were the day's sales?' Laurence asked.

'Buoyant,' she said, though his had been the only one.

A large gilt-framed mirror hung on the wall behind him. She saw Laurence's back view, foxed and blotched with marks like liver spots. The wallpaper was faded pyjama stripes, purple and grey.

'Good for you. You're obviously a natural.' Laurence started to rub his silk tie with his thumb. 'You won't remember my outdoor pub games venture. I was a callow twenty-one. I got stuffed with a garage full of giant backgammon and shove ha'penny. It was Gareth Hyssop's father's garage; a lock-up behind Curzon Street. He was quite difficult about it.' An aggrieved expression crossed

13

his face. Then, because the occasion was long past, he looked at Anita and smiled.

She began to eat bread and, when the time came, ordered darne of pollock with chorizo.

Laurence kept talking. He had a fund of stories. He had seen Izzy and Piers. He had seen Jemima, recently back from a charity trek in the Himalayas. He had bumped into Fran at the airport and recommended the archaeological museum in Varna to her.

'Was Fran going to Bulgaria?' Anita interrupted him.

'No, I was, Mossy. Weren't you listening?' Laurence replied, before resuming the flow.

He had bought a small apartment in the Dobrich region that was 'cheap as chips' and intended to 'scout' for rural properties to sell to the property-hungry English. He planned to do the same in Montenegro.

His plump face remained in the same spot in front of her like a static moon. Even when he raised his champagne glass to his mouth or stroked the back of his neck, he looked straight at her.

Anita felt both trapped and physically connected to Laurence, as if she had inadvertently married him. She tried not to talk too much and only asked questions about inanimate things like the Chalcolithic collection – repeating the word cautiously because it was new to her. She needed to be incredibly careful; if she made a wrong step she could end up in bed with him. He was one of those men who made her mind wander in that direction. She wondered what doing it with him would be like – though she didn't desire him, indeed, preferred him in an overcoat and scarf, so that as little of him was as visible as possible. She had no notion where the idea came from – whether some perversity in herself, or auto-suggestion by him – but she knew that he knew.

She ate more bread, tackled the darne of pollock and tried to keep an eye on how much champagne she was drinking, though this was difficult because the bottle was in a bucket with a white napkin round its neck. She suspected that the waiter topped up her glass whenever Laurence performed one of his habitual spasmodic actions; the fingering of the tie or the hair stroking. She refused pudding and also coffee. She thought she was managing quite well – and then suddenly found that the conversation had taken a bizarre turn.

'Drive around the countryside, get a feel for it, take some photos of rural properties. Can't fault it really. Where's the difficulty?' Laurence was saying.

'There isn't one. As such,' she said, warily.

'Good.'

'It's not my sort of thing, Larry. I promise you it isn't.'

'That doesn't matter,' he said – at his most courteous.

'Did you ask Fran to do this?' she asked.

Laurence's well-defined, rather feminine eyebrows shot up. 'No. I told you. We discussed archaeology.' He gazed intently at her. 'What's worrying you, Mossy?'

'Nothing.'

'Nothing?' He leant across the table and touched her fingertips. 'I'm not going to be there. I shall be in London and possibly Petrovac.' He pronounced the place name beautifully.

She could feel the hand – saw it blurrily out of the corner of her left eye as if it were a side plate. She was determined not to look at it. It would be withdrawn at some stage – at the latest when the bill came.

'It's not a bad place – still something of a fishing village,' he said. 'There's an eyesore down by the harbour – a defunct silo – but you can tune it out. You'll like the setting. People are too squeamish about the Balkans.'

4

At the beginning, Anita assumed that the taller friends came with Barney and the shorter ones with Mark, though this didn't hold good as a system. Her brothers did everything together and had friends in common: Simons and Charleses. Their families skied in Verbier or fished in Donegal. Both brothers talked about the Simons and Charleses with equal enthusiasm. Both poured scorn on a boy named Bizzy who was often referred to but never invited to Hampshire. Mark and Barney were fine beasts who chomped grass in rhythm and occasionally stampeded, hooves thundering as one. Their dark heads would touch as they leant over a game, or bob up and down across the fields until their legs took them out of sight.

On the occasions her brothers were home, they and their friends careered around the house and made bonfires in the rough grass by the stream at the end of the garden. Veronica drew the line at cooking for them but she kept the freezer stashed with boy-friendly sustenance that could be heated in the microwave – or, in the case of buns, defrosted.

Veronica loved having boys around. She kept track of the visitors' sporting achievements and roles in school drama; congratulated them effusively on their wicket-keeping in house cricket matches or their singing in the chorus of *Iolanthe*. She was less enamoured of later university friends. She never quite grasped who they were and continued to ask after the Simons and Charleses. She kept in touch with old house masters.

Anita sat the Common Entrance, aged eleven. It was – she knew at the time – an opportunity for partial redemption. With her pen in her hand and in a state of heightened awareness, she took half an hour to read the paper. She opted for self-sabotage. Following a few dud starts and crossings-out, she wrote nothing. With an arm shielding the blank sheets, she stroked her ponytail with her free hand and listened to the tick of the classroom clock.

The period that followed had a peculiar quality. Time passed quickly and slowly simultaneously. It was as if the house had become a stage set. Her parents were understudies who had failed to learn their lines and were improvising atrociously.

Anita said the minimum, in a bright, non-committal voice, and felt that every utterance was marked down for posterity. Her movements became lighter, she paid attention to posture and did a kind of curtsey when she bent to kiss Viking, their flat-coated retriever, or to pick up the post from the doormat. Unfortunately, she developed a problem with her jaw which she could only relieve by opening her mouth wide to release it and, although she tried to do this in private, there were moments when the compulsion was overwhelming and she 'stretched' in full view of the family.

'Is there something the matter, Anita?' Granny Randall had come to Sunday lunch.

'No, Granny.'

'She's not doing that stupid thing with her mouth, is she? Stop it, Anita,' Veronica said without looking.

'I don't think she knows she's doing it, darling,' Granny persisted.

'Of course, she does,' Veronica said. 'How could anyone not know?'

'I don't believe she does. Her eyes stay the same.'

'Her eyes stay the same?'

'It's more like a twitch.'

'But with a twitch, the eyes close up.'

'One of them. The one with the twitch. The other stays the same.'

'I don't think so, Mother. But let's drop the subject. It's ridiculously tedious.'

'Mark used to imitate the dog. When he was little. The dog yawning. He had us in stitches.' Granny chuckled, remembering.

Anita believed that ways of being and talking were handed down. Mummy and Granny Randall were two sides of the same coin and dialogue between them had an etched, metallic quality. Granny was the Queen and her mother a portcullis. With each generational jump, people became a bit less benevolent and went on more holidays, but basically, within the family, they resembled each other. Granny was kind. She was also Anita.

Anita, the younger, imagined earlier female Randalls using words like 'fustian' – the clip-clop of hooves in the background – but being otherwise recognisable. The way Veronica said 'Kingsfold' made Anita feel sick. Anita gave her address as 15 Gee's Lane, Elvham, suppressing the Kingsfold House part entirely. Hampshire, she also avoided – abolishing the county before Royal Mail got round to it. She invented Greater Andover.

Anita must have shared some of the Randall steel, though, because she survived the Common Entrance results. There wasn't a row, as such. It was more a process that dragged on for years – was, to some extent, still dragging on. If she predeceased her parents, *Here lies Anita Florence Mostyn. Failed Common Entrance* would be inscribed on her gravestone – probably translated into Latin.

She was sent to an insignificant girls' boarding school in West Sussex – St Everild's – where nail polish was overlooked and, in due course, nose studs. The school uniform colour was brown with a mustard trim and flattered no one, not even the one Japanese girl at St Everild's, who looked lovely in everything. Mark and Barney posed in their school's black and white; monochrome to her jaundiced Technicolor. They were in a silver frame and she was loose in the photograph box. Anita's friend, Fran, was the brightest girl St Everild's had ever had and the only one to go to Oxford.

5

Anita was shepherded into her parents' tiny, over-upholstered drawing room by her father, in the hybrid garb he wore on London evenings; the trousers of his City suit topped with a red jumper; on his feet, black woollen socks and leather slippers. He stooped going through the doorways, looking like a barge chugging under a low bridge. Veronica, tall for a woman, had the measure of the mews house ceilings and kept a straight back.

In spite of the formal furnishings, there was a feeling of camping in Eccleston Mews; not out-of-doors camping, but the claustrophobia of a display tent in a travel store, since the cramped rooms lacked air.

The mews house was the Mostyns' second home; the first being in Hampshire, and the third in the department of the Tarn in France. Inherited dark wood pieces were the mainstay of all three properties but in SW1 the furniture was crammed close together, its surfaces stacked with miscellaneous items that didn't fit in the tiny galley kitchen: drying-up cloths, a microwave oven, shoe-cleaning equipment in a tartan holdall, stacks of tinned dog food, in case Saxon, the current dog, accompanied the Mostyns to London.

Veronica dressed from the selection of pale, slightly grubby, silky cardigans that were stored in the upstairs drawers – and cooked ahead of time so that she was able to sit and relax over a drink. This ritual over, Anita and Howard – sufficiently inebriated – moved to the dining room. Veronica short-circuited to the kitchen to dish up.

The dining room was at the front of the house, where horses once entered and some residents now garaged a car. The Grosvenor Estate, which owned the lease, permitted a vehicle but not a window, so boldly striped curtains that had belonged to Granny Randall were permanently drawn across a pair of locked gates; an arrangement that worked well in winter but, between April and October, created a dark night of the soul. Every month or so through winter and British Summer Time, Anita sat and ate indifferent meals by artificial light.

Her parents, in their early seventies, were vigorous and capable, in no need of cosseting, yet Anita kept up the visits, as though they were older. If she left too long a gap, she got the surprise blast of Veronica's personality. Anita never gave up hoping for approval – perhaps for adoration – of a type that had eluded her.

If the Mostyn children had been a still life, her two older brothers would have been the perfect apples in the bowl and Anita one of those splashes of paint you peer at, wondering, is it a leaf, a shadow on the tablecloth, a mistake? The boys had their mother's looks. Perky dark hair, high smooth foreheads, the Randall nose, which was elegantly long and nipped in at the nostrils. Veronica found it beguiling to look at two male children and see herself gazing back.

'Bulgaria. Will you manage, Anita?' Veronica said, her eyelids flickering and then steadying.

'I expect so,' Anita replied.

She had decided to take up Laurence's offer. Trips abroad were a sign of health, weren't they? Summer sun, winter sun, fly-drives, city breaks, hen weekends, skiing, treks. 'Go for it,' Fran had said when Anita discussed the plan with her. 'Escape from your brother's wedding. Forget about Nick Halsey.' Zest for life was measured in time away.

'And who is Laurence Beament? Have you ever mentioned him?' Veronica asked.

'I don't *know* him. He's not a friend. He works for an investment bank.' Anita foresaw the next question and named one at random.

'Never heard of him,' her father said.

'What about your work?' Veronica sampled a forkful of cauliflower cheese and reached for the pepper grinder which she applied vigorously.

'I'm taking unpaid leave,' Anita said. 'There's not much happening at the gallery. We're all set for next month's exhibition.'

Veronica twitched. 'Well, the leave might be permanent when you come back.' She viewed her daughter's job in a small private art gallery as a kind of occupational therapy. It was only when Anita treated the work lightly herself that it constituted a career, or the vestiges of one.

Veronica, formerly a solicitor, worked, pro bono, for various charities, advising them on legal matters. Howard, now almost wholly retired, sat on two pension-fund committees. He had weathered deregulation in the City and maintained status; nevertheless the last twenty years had been a winding down. His retirement project, a biography of Sir George Hamilton Seymour, remained at the research stage. Many an afternoon, he exchanged diplomacy in the time of Tsar Nicholas I for a verbal tussle with Italian scoundrels and ailing women, as he set about rewriting opera synopses in good plain English. He held that Covent Garden programme notes and even the precis of Kobbé were incomprehensible. 'You're no wiser at the end than you were at the beginning. Don't you find that?' Veronica butted in, at that point, and declared that surtitles made the endeavour otiose. 'Maybe, maybe. But I enjoy the puzzle element.' Howard closeted himself in his study with his 'ghetto blaster', as he called it, and books borrowed from the London Library. Rows of boxed CDs stood on a shelf. He had started with *Aida* and was proceeding alphabetically.

A phone began to ring in the other room.

'Answer it, darling. No one minds.' Veronica, finished with the pepper grinding, had resumed eating.

Anita got up from the table, woozy from fast drinking. She went into the drawing room and located the phone, deep inside her bag. As she picked it up, the ringing stopped. One missed call. A text message followed.

'It might be a sale, Anita. Ring them back. Close the door, if you don't want us to hear.' Veronica raised her voice so that it carried into the next room.

'Sale?' Anita said, returning.

'Your Bulgarian gîtes. You might have a buyer.' Veronica, as always, was ahead of the game.

'It was Nick Halsey,' Anita said. 'He and Emma want me to meet up with them before I leave.'

'So you *are* definitely going?' Veronica scrutinised her.

'Halsey, that's the one. I liked that man,' Howard said.

Veronica straightened herself up. 'Mark was always a good picker of friends. Not a dud among them.' She fixed her daughter with another look. 'I hadn't realised you kept in touch with Nick Halsey.'

'I haven't. I met him in April. At a lunch party,' Anita

replied. 'That was the first time after – I don't know – twenty years?'

'Where does he live these days?' Veronica asked.

'They've just bought a house near Wandsworth Common. Emma's expecting a baby. They used to live in Euston.'

'How unusual,' Veronica said.

'It wasn't that unusual.' Anita thought of the high ceilings, the racket of the traffic; buses roaring past.

Nick had driven Anita back from Izzy and Piers's house-warming party in Sussex. He had turned off the main road into Ashdown Forest and stopped the car in a copse. Naturally warm towards Mark's little sister, Nick hadn't become noticeably warmer – though it was quite possible Anita had become obtuse. If he had changed in some way – become fierce or nervy or put on a special smile – it might not have happened, but he stayed his usual charming self. He said nothing, or at least nothing of any significance. Only the movement of his right hand to the top button of his trousers alerted her. Under the birch trees, in a wooded byway, she had found the gesture oddly innocent.

She was inclined to see her part as another of her acquiescences. Men – more than women, she thought – were opportunistic. They couldn't wait to fill a gap. Afterwards, Nick had started the engine and turned on *Poetry Please* on Radio 4. Anita burrowed into the car seat. The first poem was called 'Garden Shed' and Anita hoped there would be no mention of love.

She wondered whether the gap, in that instance, had been created by Nick's girlfriend, Emma, having a stomach bug – or whether she herself had become a kind of void. When the traffic seized up as they approached the M25 junction, Nick called Emma on his mobile and explained that he was at a standstill on the A22. Essentially this was true. Anita knew how these things were done; the gross omissions.

Inevitably, the minor detour wasn't a one-off. Nick's Thursday-afternoon meetings with the communications planning people took on another dimension – and a little more time. He left the meetings early and arrived home slightly late. Emma remained the fixed point. Anita was not the fixed point, he said. Transgressive enough to be fun, she thought. Mark's little sister.

Howard half rose from his chair, picked up the bottle and refilled the wine glasses. He moved stiffly these days. His hand had a slight tremor. It jiggered like the unseasonal fly that buzzed in one of the curtains, fussing between the folds.

'Are the houses picturesque? I imagine they might be,' Veronica asked.

'They're gradually being made over. Most still have masses of bells,' Anita said.

'Bells. How delightful. Some miniature campanile arrangement? I thought maybe whitewash, overhanging tiles. The odd dovecote,' Veronica said.

'Oh, sorry. I see what you mean. I was in Euston. Actually I wasn't. I wasn't anywhere. No, I really don't know. I've never been to Bulgaria,' Anita said.

'*Not* on my list of must-see places.' Veronica chuckled.

She gazed at Anita as if trying to work out her daughter's motivation.

'Food's fairly monotonous, I should think. But so it is in Greece.' Howard wiped his mouth with his napkin and took another gulp of wine.

'Will you be any *good* at negotiation?' Veronica asked.

'I'm taking pictures – for the website.' Anita said. 'I drive around the countryside looking for likely houses. They don't have to be for sale. They're bait to lure the clients.'

'How peculiar.' Howard frowned.

'But seriously. Timing, darling. Kendra's birthday on the thirtieth of October and then the wedding in November.'

Anita greeted the dates with silence. Her brother Barney was getting married. He and Kendra had a website: barneyandkendragetmarried.com. It contained all the wedding details and at the end, after the map of

Elvham, was a clock that ticked off the minutes, hours and days. Anita tantalised herself by looking at it, wondering whether she had the nerve not to turn up – to stay away in Bulgaria. The numbers on the clock continued to roll. Anita was powerless to stop them. It was her brother's second marriage but Kendra's first, which was why the fuss was happening. No one had considered Anita's feelings.

She said, 'I won't be around for the birthday. Kendra's. I'm leaving next week.'

'Why do you say it like that? *Kendra's.*' Veronica gave a fairly accurate imitation.

'I suppose because I have arrested development.' Anita bit her lip.

Veronica ignored the comment and, for a while, talked of other things, though she had a feverish look. Howard manfully chewed the pieces of the previous day's roast potatoes that his wife had sliced up and added to the cauliflower. He occasionally nodded. The fly had settled down, asleep on the curtain.

Anita waited. Veronica could hold several conversations at the same time; though only one was audible. Her facial expressions and demeanour followed a different argument which she would return to. She gathered pace on the subject of a local planning application, before interrupting herself. 'Wouldn't it be better to postpone your trip till the New Year, Anita? This does seem rather rushed.'

Howard laid down his fork in the pool of cheese sauce. 'It's not Ush-Terek, Ronnie. She's not being exiled.'

6

Lots Road Power Station loomed over the street and over Cremorne Gardens, the tiny park by the Thames that was a three-minute walk from Anita's flat. A concrete jetty on hefty wooden piers stretched into the water. Occasionally, in the daytime, boys came to fish. Anita enjoyed the vista of Chelsea Old Church, Battersea Old Church, river mud, distant bridges. With selective looking, she blocked out the new developments that stretched along the Thames. Trucks rumbled in the background. Veronica loathed the power station and was convinced that right-thinking types would demolish it. The two towers seemed kindly to Anita. Returning home, she was always glad to see them.

Her flat was a conversion; the ground floor of an Edwardian terraced house, in a part of Chelsea where there was perpetual heavy traffic. Cars and lorries swung round away from the Embankment into Gunter Grove, like an outfalling sewer, and the little roads off to the west, of which Anita's was one, heard its rush, day and night, though cut off from the flow. She had occasional panics that the traffic would miss the bend and hurtle her way. And then there was the dirt – she lived behind grimy windows. Dust coated the sills and the mouldings on the lintel.

Veronica and Howard, who wanted to see their daughter settled, had helped her to buy the flat – the SW10 postcode was on the fringe of acceptable. That was what prosperous parents did and Anita was grateful for the assistance. She had been there for years; first renting with Gavin Peace and then as an owner. Friends moved up the property ladder, acquiring children and new kitchens. She couldn't help comparing herself with them and noticing a lack of progress.

She was lucky, though. The general stasis, or downward drift in relation to her peers, was a matter of perception. Most of the time, she was happy, or happy enough. She shut the door on household problems when she set out for work; the kitchen drain that was partly blocked, the faulty automatic ignition on the cooker. Her paperwork remained chaotic. She hadn't yet looked at her tax return but was resolved to do so before she went to Bulgaria. She also planned an autumn clear-out.

In common with the Mostyn houses, Anita's Chelsea flat was cluttered. Clothes accumulated; some new and still in their bags; others strewn over chairs. Drawers were so stuffed that they no longer closed. Garment sleeves hung out of them like arms tired from fruitless SOS signalling. Slippery exhibition catalogues from the gallery and back copies of art magazines balanced in uneven piles. Anita was always tripping over things. Indian artefacts that belonged to Gavin Peace – the gong and the carved wooden figures, the stone chapatti dishes they had once used as ashtrays – lived an afterlife she had never got round to expunging. Other boyfriends had left token stuff: paperbacks and CDs; items of clothing. Miles Greener's swimming trunks had turned up, among dustballs under the bath. Gavin's relinquishment had been more thorough. His complete works of Jung kept an eye on her from the bookshelves. Certain titles demoralised her; Alan Watts's *Seeds of Genius*, for example. Genius was not a word she wanted down the spine of a paper-back. Its flyleaf was inscribed, *For Anita – All love, Gav*, in Gavin's spiky handwriting. Knowing his habit of giving her books that he wanted himself, she should have been able to give the book away to Oxfam – but hadn't. Gav had waived attachment to things – and so had she, in theory. It perplexed her that eight years later she was still surrounded by his stuff while he had got clean away.

Gav had been older, thirty-one to her twenty-two, when they got together; too old to show promise, forever on a brink. He would ring out of the blue and say, 'Meet me in Lahore,' which was fun up to a point, and though cheap flights were available, getting to the place at short notice was usually impossible. Once, Anita turned up at a hotel in Acapulco and Gav had moved on. Her not joining him was always an excuse for whatever happened next.

In spite of his absences, the time with Gavin had had a sunny quality. He had been different from the Mostyns with their evident perfections. They all – including Mark and Barney – regarded him as some kind of joke. Gav had steered clear of them. He never would go to Hampshire. He despised kinship and cited Colin Wilson. When the relationship ended Anita read his falling-to-pieces copy of *The Outsider*. She failed to find any of the lines Gav had quoted and assumed she had missed them – lacking the intelligence to home in on the sparky bits. She had a single reading pace – *lento doloroso*, Veronica called it. Passages that other people skipped slowed her down. She read every word.

There had been lovers after Gavin, though they left less vivid impressions. Anita needed to cross-check a mental diary to get sequences right. After each split from a boyfriend, she became least satisfactory Mostyn again; some kind of Mostyn, anyway. She wasn't a born outsider; not existentially, more by default. She still hoped to become more scintillating.

*

The Sunday before she was due to leave, Anita met Nick and Emma for late breakfast at a café overlooking Wandsworth Common. It was one of those days, clear and sharp, when autumn seems a kind of spring. There were other people, whom Anita didn't know; James, in a camel coat, Stella, a child in a buggy. Croissants arrived and the little boy stopped screaming.

'This Friday? That's really, really soon.' Emma jumped in surprise.

She was wearing a princess-style coat that hid the curve of her belly.

'The skiing is supposed to be good,' James said. 'Bansko, isn't it?'

'We'll come and get you if you stay too long, won't we?' Emma said. 'Nicholas?'

He had tipped the café chair back and turned his head towards the common. He was wearing the old jacket with frayed cuffs that he wore at weekends and a wool scarf that Emma had knitted for him. The trees were full of golden leaves with as many again scattered in drifts on the grass. Children ran through them, scuffing them up.

'Yes, I'll fetch her,' Nick said.

'It wouldn't occur to me to buy in Bulgaria; Slovenia, possibly,' James said.

'I've heard of Bansko,' Stella said, pulling apart another croissant.

'I hope you meet lots and lots of lovely people,' Emma said. 'Will there be any?'

'I don't know.' Anita picked at threads of wool where her scarlet fingerless gloves were fraying.

To Emma, she was the sister of an old friend of Nick's: Anita Mostyn who had turned up at Izzy and Piers's house-warming. The 'little' would not be relevant, since Anita was older than Emma. The friend, Mark Mostyn, was dead. Nick must have told Emma that. Emma was always nice to Anita, knowing, probably, nothing about her but this single fact. The death of any young person was shocking. She was a sweet-natured woman – guileless. She included Anita in their circle.

A bus stopped and blocked the view but Nick continued to look towards the common as though he had special object-penetrating sight.

'There's all that trouble in Spain. Land grab. The mayor comes with a bulldozer and totals your villa,' James said. 'Does that happen in Bulgaria? Everything belongs to distant uncles, doesn't it? You can probably buy them off.'

'November's early for skiing,' Stella said, passing a flaky chunk of croissant down to the opening fist.

'I'm not going to the mountains,' Anita said. 'I'm going to the Black Sea.'

'Come straight back if you're lonely. She must, mustn't

she, Nicholas?' Emma adjusted her beret. The bus had moved on. 'Nicholas, darling, what is so interesting over there?'

'Looks like a ginger Labrador. You don't often see one of those,' James said.

Nick caught Anita's eye. He looked at her steadily and she had no idea what he was thinking.

7

He came to stay in the summer vacation of Mark's first year at Cambridge and Barney's second. The wheels of a car crunched on the drive. The front door slammed, loud enough to set the dog barking, and then Anita heard footsteps and laughing, Mark's going off in bursts, like gunfire.

Nothing could have dragged Anita to the window. She remained sitting on her bed, combing her wet hair. It was shoulder-length in those days, the colour of cheesy maize snacks; darker and more plausible when wet. She hated it; both the thin straggliness and the vile colour. Her school trunk was open on the floor, part unpacked, reeking of the gym changing room. She waited, listening to clatterings up the stairs and male voices; later the retreat down and through the house. The voices switched off. Mark and the friend had gone into the garden. She hoped to make an entrance, only it would be more of an exit via the open back door – and then what?

An hour later, barefoot and wearing dance leggings under a short lime green skirt, her hair scraped back under a wide black band, Anita appeared.

The boys were at the far end of the lawn, sunning themselves with their shirts off. A wine bottle stood between them. Mark was talking. He sat cross-legged and leaned forward in combative posture – intent on what he was saying. The friend lazed, reclining on his elbows. Every now and then, he stretched out a hand and picked up the bottle. He took a swig and passed it to Mark. He squinted into the sun through half-closed eyes and seemed to enjoy the weather. He looked at home in the world. At that distance, he lacked detail but Anita could tell he was more normal than her brother.

Anita, thirteen years old, stood in the open doorway. She couldn't just go up to them. Neither could she stand and stare for ever, waiting for the friend's next lazy movement. In the shadow of the house, she set off in an anti-clockwise direction, thinking this more mysterious than simply retreating inside. The paving slabs were hot. She kept close to the walls and went slowly but nonchalantly, looking at the ground. Every inch was familiar to her.

In her mind she heard, 'Hey, Netticles, have you lost something?' She stepped over the hose, coiled like a cobra, and skirted round Viking's water bowl. But the call never came. Mark affected not to have seen her. She hated that. With every step she got younger. She headed back towards childhood.

She reached the corner and continued searching, along

the side of the building, though the boys could no longer see her. By then, she believed her own story and pushed her bare foot into weedy clumps at the bottom of the brickwork, dislodging stones, a colony of ants and one rusty hairpin.

When she reached the front door she found it unexpectedly locked. Shut out, she was confirmed in her belief that she didn't belong in Kingsfold House and never had done. The option of returning to the back door she rejected as demeaning. She hitched up the skirt and pulled herself on to the sill of one of the long windows. Once evenly balanced, she cupped her hands and peered through the glass. Everything was at an odd angle. The rigid lines imposed by their cleaner – rugs squared up, little tables made parallel, *The Spectator* precisely on top of *The Economist* – looked better seen obliquely, more like a picture. It was a real room, though, not a painting. The sofa cushions had been dented since the cleaner's visit.

Anita pushed on the glazing bars and raised the window. It creaked and rattled over the sashes. She crouched in the gap, then jumped.

'You look like a tropical bird that's lost its way,' Mark's friend said, coming in through the drawing-room door. 'Do you by any chance have a match? I seem to have lost my lighter.'

41

She looked at him – at the smooth, sculpted flesh between his ribcage and his navel.

'Mine's upstairs. I could get it . . .' she said.

Anita was too young to buy cigarettes, though she did, occasionally. She was also – cruelly – three years below the age of consent. Did that seriously bother anyone? She was wearing bright colours. She had flown through the window.

'There's also a box of matches in the log basket if you don't want to wait,' she said. 'They'll be damp but just keep trying. I expect one will spark up.'

'Thank you. Good thinking,' the friend said. 'Who are you?'

'Anita.'

She suppressed the word sister.

'Anita,' he repeated.

The name swelled in her head – then shrank to the size of a raisin.

'I'm Nick,' he said.

Veronica, Howard and Barney were up in London all that week; Veronica and Howard in Belgravia, Barney staying with his old friend Charlie Burroughs. In the garden of Kingsfold House, empty wine bottles accumulated under the Indian bean tree. Invisible for most of the day, they caught the light in the later part of the afternoon. Anita had the house to herself but no use for it. Viking abandoned her. He preferred to be outside, lying next to the boys. Occasionally, Nick Halsey or Mark came in from the garden to fetch something. The dog would follow.

Nick moved quietly like a fox. Anita never knew where she might come across him. He smiled in a friendly way but she made no impression on him. She should never have mentioned damp matches. Fran despaired of her when they played 'Associations'. 'Mossy, you are so prosaic. This is meant to be fun! How can "thong" make you think of "apple core"?' Anita had undone all the good of her dramatic entrance. She kept to her room and felt suffocated. The scent of marijuana wafted in through the window.

Barney and her parents turned up on Friday evening. Barney with a girl called Tasha, whom no one, including Barney, seemed particularly interested in.

Veronica was casually hospitable. The message was, 'Help yourself, but this is my house and the end of my week.'

She didn't go out of her way to be pally with Nick Halsey, as she had with the Simons and Charleses of her sons' schooldays. She proclaimed the ineptitude of various colleagues and opened her post. Howard dispensed drinks and talked about politics.

The boys and Tasha went out to a pub in Nick's car.

Anita couldn't believe that her parents failed to notice the lingering scent of dope.

'Can't you smell anything?' she asked, holding her nose.

'No,' Veronica said. 'I don't spend my time sniffing.'

The empties had vanished from the lawn.

On Saturday, after a late start, Mark and Nick drove off for the day. It was an abrupt departure that didn't allow for discussion. One moment, the chaos of breakfast – burnt toast, stewed tea, the news and sports sections of the newspapers bagged, the supplements discarded – the next, the rev of a car engine. Viking, half asleep in front of the oven, opened one eye and closed it again.

Anita, in her black and white cowhide print dressing gown, tightly belted, with only knickers beneath it, pulled at strands of wet hair. She twiddled them into corkscrews and unwound them again as she looked at the fashion pages. She was relieved, in a way, to have Nick Halsey whipped away from her. Glimpses were unsettling. She would spend the day preparing for an evening sighting; her fantasy existence fed by fragments.

'Where has Mark gone?' Barney asked.

Howard and Veronica were deep in the papers. Howard grunted occasionally. Tasha was poking around in the cupboards. Anita wondered how long it would take her to find the coffee, which lived in an old red tin marked 'Cocoa'.

'Mum, where have they gone?' Barney said, with his sad teddy bear face on. He biffed the *Financial Times* that was shielding Veronica.

'Oh, for goodness' sake, Barney. Whatever's the matter?' Veronica said.

He repeated the question.

'I've no idea, darling. You should have asked him.' She disappeared again.

Barney looked mournful, as though someone had died. Tasha was washing her hands at the sink, scrubbing off the stickiness, the fine film of grease, she had encountered in the cupboards. She looked around for a clean towel; gingerly parted the drying-up cloths and encrusted oven gloves on the rail of the oven, then wiped her hands on the back of her jeans. She went into the larder. Opening the door released a pent-up smell of Stilton. Viking woke up, shook himself, and followed her in.

Anita, who had thought Tasha spineless, changed her mind. As well as being seriously addicted to caffeine, the girl was persistent. She seemed to have realised that there was no point in asking Mostyns for help.

'I think they took towels,' Anita said.

'What's that, Netticles?' Barney said.

'They were carrying towels. Perhaps they've gone to the sea.'

'Did you hear that, Mum? Netticles says they've gone to the sea.'

'Mm?' Veronica said.

'Well, that's not fair, is it? I mean, supposing we wanted to go to the sea. They could at least have asked.' Barney droned on for about ten minutes. No one responded. It was a beautiful July day. The sun warmed the kitchen.

For the remaining days that Nick Halsey stayed, Barney became a human dowsing rod that tracked Mark's whereabouts. The garden wasn't private enough: Barney came lumbering over with Tasha trailing behind him. Mark and Nick went out in Nick's car or hid in Mark's room. It became a den of perpetual evening in summer weather. Music and muffled laughter seeped out through the gap under the closed door. The two of them stayed there for hours and what they said or did was a mystery. The window that overlooked the garden offered no clues. A half-drawn curtain. Anita couldn't help thinking that Mark's possessiveness of Nick Halsey was a touch over-managed. In Howard and Veronica's absence, the dope smoking got going again.

Barney borrowed his mother's car and went to play

golf, leaving Tasha in the drawing room, leafing through back copies of *The Economist*, as though she were at the dentist. He had no success in getting up group outings, but, one afternoon, Nick and Mark emerged and, of their own free will, suggested a game of poker. Clear-eyed and polite, neither had a whiff of the nightclub about them.

They set up a card table in the garden under the trees. The three boys laughed together. Tasha was the one who kept yawning. She looked like yesterday's candle, more drip than wick, and kept losing money.

8

The Friday after meeting Nick and Emma at the café by Wandsworth Common, Anita flew to Bulgaria. She arrived in Varna in the early evening and took a taxi from the airport to Laurence's fishing village forty miles north. She told the driver she wanted The Hesperia and after slowing down outside other developments further along the coast, he finally delivered her to a new building that stood alone on a tract of land large enough for several apartment blocks.

Isolated as it was, The Hesperia seemed unanchored. Raw, yellow brickwork emerged wonkily from bands of shadow. The staggered balconies, lit from beneath by external up-lighters, hung precariously. In a high wind they might all come crashing down.

Anita shut the cab door, paid the fare and dragged her suitcase up to the curved glass entrance; the wheels caught the edge of each step.

There was no one in the lobby. A small palm tree in a large pot stood on the polished tiles, its upended image reflected in the shine. A desk was at one end of the long room, at the other a bar, empty of bottles, curved in a semicircle, surrounded by red-topped bar stools.

Anita see-sawed from the plane and the bumpy taxi ride. She pushed a glass door and set off along a walkway, or open gallery, that bordered a courtyard, trundling the suitcase between pillars and interrupting the silence. Above her, balconies curved like interlocking surfboards. She re-entered a different part of the building. Ground floor, Laurence had said, so she ignored a lift and a flight of concrete stairs and carried on. Identical doors were spaced at intervals down the corridor; laminate-coated, with a chrome number and a spyhole like a tiny glass eye. Eight, seven, six . . . Anita stopped at door three. The key clicked in the lock.

Once inside, she switched on the lights and left her bag in the small hallway. Taints of new materials had accumulated in the closed space. There was no whiff of Laurence's own particular smell. She went from room to room and could have been in any new apartment or hotel suite. Views of the Indian Ocean – or Bayswater Road – might have been hidden behind the drawn blinds. The ceilings were too low to produce an echo; instead, the white-painted walls gave a dead bounce that muted the sound of her footsteps as she crossed the floor. All the furnishings were standard items suitable for rental property: beige sofas, circular cotton rugs, wood-framed mirrors. Laurence hadn't imposed his taste – whatever the equivalent of leopard-print ties was in interiors.

She hadn't seen him again after the Chelsea dinner. He had backed off, merely sending instructions by email and the keys in a bubble-wrap envelope. At her request, he had arranged for a hire car to be delivered to The Hesperia. She hadn't wanted to find her way, in the dusk, from the airport. *NB: the kitchen tap. Pull. Don't twist. No rush for the photographs. Enjoy*, Laurence had added.

Anita recalled the pictures on The Hesperia's website, taken on improbably sparkling days from advantageous positions. The Black Sea was a startling blue in the background. She had taken the virtual tour of the show flat, gliding from room to room, computer mouse under her hand, lulled by the cartoon simplicity and restricted colour palette. Looking about her now, she decided reality was better, though she missed the neat black outlines around the furniture and fittings. The feeling of being a bit out of it, as if she were floating, was still with her.

The galley-shaped, windowless kitchen was on a kind of stage to one side of the main room. Anita went up the steps and switched on the lights. An extractor fan began to whir. Intending to make herself some tea, she picked up the kettle and took it to the sink. The tap squeaked but nothing came out. Water rationing, she thought, and gave the tap a final smack. A cascade whooshed over her, drenching her legs. 'Retard,' she said aloud.

Leaving the kettle to boil, she returned to the living room. On her phone were text messages from various people: Fran, Laurence, her mother, Emma and Nick as a joint enterprise. Niels had sent a clip of himself, waving his scarf in some pastiche of a folk dance. Everyone hoped she had arrived safely and wished her luck. *I'm here!* she replied. *Love the apartment. Can't wait to see the sea.*

Anita unlocked the patio doors and stepped outside. The sky was a series of blue-greens in horizontal bands, like a paint chart. She could have been anywhere – almost. The defining categories were broad. Somewhere temperate; the autumn damp. Near the sea; the recognisable tang. A hedge bordered the terrace. Knee-high, trimmed flat, it invited something to be placed on it – a tray with a glass on, or a plate of something to pick at. Its dense leaves that made it seem load-bearing would one day provide privacy. Swimmers dipping in and out of the water would be moving specks of colour behind a green screen.

The pool, the focal point of the development, being dry, late in the season, reflected nothing. It was an inverted mould, like a giant piece of kitchen equipment that had lodged itself in the ground. On the far side, a series of apartment windows were dotted with white putty marks, as if work were still in progress. Anita looked up, searching for signs of life behind the balconies.

At around seven thirty, her phone rang.

'Hullo. How are you?' The voice was husky, slightly muffled, as though the sound came through a sock.

Anita returned to the lobby. She hurried along the corridors, clutching her phone. Through plate glass, she saw two identical cars parked in front of The Hesperia, one with a driver. The forecourt, a bland half-circle of tarmac, was sliced into segments by the building's lighting. A man stood at the foot of the steps.

'Hullo-how-are-you?' was repeated, the words run together, as she emerged through the doors.

The engine of the occupied car was running. The man on the step carried on smoking while completing the paperwork. He raised a knee as a temporary table, then gave the document to Anita to sign in two places. He handed her keys.

The car bounced away down the road, the red tail lights intermittently obscured by a plume of exhaust fumes. Its twin remained in the middle of the tarmac. Anita returned to the lobby, approached the desk and pressed the bell. She waited and tried again, gazing at the internal door to the office, as if the frosted glass would suddenly light up and produce the silhouette of a porter. She was about to give up and go back to the apartment for Laurence's instructions when she heard footsteps and the squeak of a shoe.

'Hi. I've been ringing for the porter. Do you think he's gone home?' Anita said, addressing the man who was walking across the lobby.

'As far as I know, there isn't a porter,' the man said.

'Someone's delivered a hired car for me and left it at the front.'

'Well, it might get stolen. You should move it to the secure car park,' he said.

The man was heftily built, middle-aged and suntanned. He wore pale chinos and a black shirt undone to the third button. His hair, swept back from his forehead like a mane, was the colour of tarnished pound coins.

'Where is it, the secure car park?' she asked.

'It's pretty straightforward. Take a left round the side of the block. Keep going, keep going. You see the security gates ahead. Use your key fob to get in. Everything's out of doors; nothing underground here.'

'Left, did you say?'

He glanced at her. 'I'll show you where to go, if you like.'

'That's really kind. Thank you,' she said.

53

They went out through the double glass doors and down the curved steps edged with twinkling lights. He put his arm out behind her, shepherding her. They exchanged names. Anita, Connor.

9

The interior of the car was cramped and smelled of cigarette smoke and peach air-freshener. The driver's seat was still warm. Connor wound the window down. All Anita could see in the murky hollow below the console were legs; his in the lightweight chinos, hers in skinny jeans. She adjusted the seat from its boy racer position so that she was sitting upright and further forward. The leg situation changed; less like the dodgems.

Anita inserted the key in the ignition, started the engine and, after a few false moves that caused the windscreen wipers to labour across dry glass, switched the headlamps on. She executed every step with long gaps in between as if someone were giving her bad instructions. Connor shifted in his seat.

Anita took a breath. She put the car in gear and took the handbrake off. Because the ground was level they didn't move. She laughed. 'Sorry, I'm pathetic with new cars,' she said.

'Take your time,' Connor replied.

The headlamps lit up a section of tarmac and the

scrubby land adjacent to it. Here and there thorny spikes of seaside plants poked through the sandy soil. The engine chugged pointlessly.

Anita felt clammy, though a breeze came in through the open window. Beyond the patch of tarmac lit by the headlamps, she could just make out the land ahead: flat, free of landmarks, it stretched to a dark, duny ridge that hid the sea. Wispy things moved in the foreground.

Her hands gripped the steering wheel at the ten to two position. Small pale knuckles. No rings. Unbitten thumbnails. Holding tight, she stared ahead and seemed dissociated from her feet, in pink plimsolls, that were as braced as her hands, the left clamped on the clutch, the right poised on the accelerator.

Anita was aware that she was being ridiculous – and appeared ridiculous to the stranger beside her. She tried to concentrate, but that ability had gone, as had the one that allowed relaxation. She was somehow freewheeling, but in a way that was highly stressful, as if all the good brakes were off and more sinister restrictions applied. With her head rigid, benumbed by anxiety, she tried to unglue her hands but they wouldn't budge. Inaction was turning into something done to her, heavy as stones – more like paralysis. The car interior was caving in; a swelling here, a crease there. She needed to speak but her throat, linked to the rhythmic beat of her chest, dried up. The air began to spin, slowly at first then faster; circling like a cat in a diminishing basket. From far away she heard a cough.

A shadow moved across the console and a thud, indistinguishable from the shadow, startled her. Anita jerked forward, her foot on the accelerator. The car bounced. It shot to the end of the driveway. The front wheels scraped the scrubby soil and she pulled the steering wheel round with a wild overcorrection. They were heading for the entrance steps. Reflected headlamps loomed in the glass doors of the lobby and suddenly there were lights everywhere; strong lights from different directions, like ambulances converging.

'Brake, fucking brake, girl. Left foot down.'

Then darkness as simple as breaking an egg into a bowl.

Anita's forehead was resting on the steering wheel. The engine was silent – stalled.

'Do you want to swap places?' someone said.

'No, it's cool.' She was trembling. 'Yes please.'

She opened the car door and got out, trying to control the shaking. The apartment block stood solid and still. An orange light winked from the top of a lorry as it moved along the main road.

Behind her, doors slammed, an engine was started. She heard a car reverse fast in a competent curve across the tarmac. For a moment, she was caught in the red glow of its tail lights. She turned and saw a large man in the driver's seat. Connor. She recalled him now and remembered his name. The car vanished round the corner of the building.

After a few minutes, Anita followed, both disembodied and with too much body, not knowing what she was doing; moving as through a strange liquid – an elderly breast-stroke, with her head above thick water.

The car slowed and stopped in front of a pair of security gates set in a high mesh fence. Connor waited until she caught up, then his arm emerged from the window. The opening mechanism clicked and the gates slid apart. She hurried through as he turned into a parking bay and brought the car to a stop.

'I'm really, really sorry,' she said, when she reached him.

'No worries.' Connor locked the car and handed her the keys.

'Let's go back,' she said.

They crossed the car park diagonally, aiming for a side entrance into the building. Anita padded along beside Connor, her hands still quivering.

'My driving instructor was nuts,' Connor said, breaking the silence.

'Really?'

Connor cleared his throat. 'Actually there were two of them, Duncan and Hayes. Hayes was learning. He sat in the front.'

Anita looked up at him.

'I'm talking back in the day. I was seventeen. Couldn't wait to get my licence. They were a rum couple. Some weird hate vibe was going on between them.' Connor paused. 'One particular lesson – I've never forgotten – I was coming up to a big roundabout on the Great North Road. Duncan calls out from the back, "In the next few minutes, I won't say when, Hayes will say 'Stop' and tap the dashboard." And I'm thinking, this isn't the place for an emergency stop. Way too much traffic. He's testing Hayes. I'll just keep driving. I look in the mirror and Duncan's eyes are kind of piercing the back of Hayes's head. Neither of them is taking a blind bit of notice of me. I keep going. Nothing happens, nothing happens. I'm getting a bit edgy . . .'

Connor stopped speaking. They had reached an entrance at the back of the building. He passed the key fob over the sensor and opened the door. Anita followed him in. They were in a lobby; the cleaners' domain. The walls were unplastered, lit by a flickering neon tube. A broom and mop bucket stood in a corner and emitted a strong smell of bleach.

'You sure you're OK?' Connor said.

'Did I scream?' she asked.

'Not really,' he said. 'Like a small scream.' He parted his lips as if he might try an imitation, and thought better of it. 'It was like nearly drowning in a paddling pool. I didn't know you could go so fast in first gear.' Connor smiled.

Anita tried one in response and, instead, dropped the clutch of keys she was holding. They fell with a clink on the floor.

'You were telling me something; a story,' she said.

'Forget it. It was stupid,' he said.

'No, it wasn't.'

Connor bent down. His hair flopped forward. She saw grey at the roots where hair dye had grown out. He straightened up again, and handed the keys to her.

'Where's your apartment?' he asked.

'On the ground floor.'

'I'll see you back there.'

They went along the passage and came out on the pillared walkway.

'It's the pick of the development down here. I'm upstairs,' Connor said. 'My apartment's finished to Bulgarian National Standard. That is, not finished: concrete floors, unpainted walls, no fixtures or fittings. You probably had more sense than to go in for that.'

'I don't own the apartment, sadly. It belongs to a friend,' Anita said. 'It's definitely been decorated, though. I can smell the paint.'

'You can relax, then. Enjoy your holiday,' he said.

When they reached Laurence's corridor, the lights, operated by a timed sensor, came on. The walls converged towards vanishing point; the apartment doors like blank pages in a book.

'This is it. Thank you so much,' Anita said.

'You'll be all right? Connor looked down at her.

She nodded.

He hesitated, awkward. 'I shouldn't have done that. Sorry,' he said. 'It was a bit . . . you know . . . stronger than I intended.' He paused. 'I got like, kind of . . .' He raised his hands and made them vibrate. His teeth were clenched in mock frustration. 'Luckily, no harm done, was there? Mind yourself,' he said and turned before she was able to reply.

She heard his feet going back along the corridor, then pounding up the concrete stairs; one flight, two flights. She lost count.

10

Anita gathered up the duvet. It smelled faintly chemical, as did the whole apartment. She carried it out through the open doors and draped it over the garden table, exposing it to the autumn sun. The day was empty. It had the emptiness of private galleries when no one comes in to look round. The Hesperia was sunk in weekend silence.

She went back inside to put an extra jumper on and to collect a mug of tea, her book and her sunglasses. She was conscious of her movements; partly because of the stillness around her, partly because her head seemed to be set on her spine like a precariously balanced bowl. This was new; caused, maybe, by a minor form of whiplash, as a result of the driving fiasco.

Out on the terrace again, she manoeuvred two of the matching garden chairs that were propped against the table. She sat down gingerly on one and placed her feet on the second, making a V-shape with her legs on which to prop the book.

If reading were a destination both into and away from

herself, Anita didn't get there. The words hung in a strange, uncomfortable space. Apartment windows surrounded her, some slashed by sunlight, some in shade. She was aware of the other private terraces that stretched to her left and right – and their mirror images on the far side of the empty swimming pool. Each was a discrete pocket, separated by low evergreen hedging. Whenever Anita looked up – slowly because of the neck – she saw a folded recliner, protected by a waterproof cover, that stood several plots away. She was the other random vertical. She felt oversize, as though she had strayed into a miniature garden. After a chapter of automatic page turning, she gave up.

She switched on her iPod and sang snatches of song as she washed up the mug and tidied up the few items that were lying about in the living room: an empty plastic water bottle, a pair of plimsolls, the previous day's newspaper. Overhandled and drained of content, the newspaper had recycled itself on the journey and was now inside out and criss-crossed with fold lines. She moved between the rooms and her flip-flops produced a delayed, plucked sound, as though some annoying toy were following her, out of sync with the music.

There was nothing to anchor her in the clean, borrowed apartment. She picked up the keys and went out, closing the front door behind her. She walked down the long corridor and out again into the courtyard that was pillared like a cloister, then back inside, along the passage. She retraced her steps of the previous evening. Finally, she arrived at the lobby that contained the broom and the bucket and the back door to the car park.

The Fiat was lined up neatly, where Connor had left it, with its bonnet towards the black school-style mesh. Anita crossed the tarmac, unlocked the driver's door and slipped into the seat with staged carelessness. She switched on the engine. Her feet, in the flip-flops, gripped the ridged mat, rubber on rubber, touching neither the clutch nor the brakes. She knew about panic. She had had attacks in the past – though not for years – and never in a car. On one occasion, she had been on a packed train to Woking, another time in a hospital lift. Both incidents had taken place in a crush of people – and ended in faints. She was mortified that the difficulty had re-emerged and fastened itself to her sole means of getting about.

As her heartbeat quickened, she closed her eyes and tried to imagine herself back in her old blue Peugeot that was parked in the road in SW10. Children on silvery scooters tore past on the pavement, their legs scooping the air. Traffic roared along the Embankment. Nothing was as loud as the thud in her chest. She sat there, her hands locked on the steering wheel, slippery with sweat. Her legs trembled.

She got out of the car and clung to the mesh to steady herself. In daylight, the sandy landscape was revealed: the ruched dunes that stretched towards the sea and, on a rising turn, hid it from view. No one was around to witness her – a lone figure wearing bright colours. She took a few deep breaths of sea air and had another go. Open the door, slip into the seat, switch on the engine. This time she recalled driving in Ireland. The lane was narrow. A horse grazed in a nearby field and the smell of cow parsley came through the open car window. She had gone on holiday with Matt Woodall who twisted his ankle coming down the steps of the plane at Knock airport. A lapsed Catholic, he had tried a hilarious genuflexion and come to grief – though the injury wasn't what had gone wrong with the holiday. The memory held for seconds then lost focus. Her breathing accelerated to the point of gasping, but she didn't go through the full panic sequence. Something protected her from it; some heavy force within herself. It didn't feel like kindly protection.

On the main road, billboards offered new property for sale further down the coast. The pictures were of completed Black Sea developments; sparkling buildings set against azure sea. Cars passed and Anita, heading for the harbour on foot, stepped aside under the hoardings. There were no landmarks; nothing but scrubby land waiting to be built on and developments in the early stages of construction. One day, other buildings like The Hesperia would rise up with their full complement of lifts, floor tiles, downlighters, gold-tipped railings, evergreen hedges.

After about twenty minutes, she reached the beginning of the town. She passed single-storey prefabs with boarded-up windows, chicken runs, sleeping dogs, leaning walls that were patched up with plaster. The kerbstones were steep and uneven. She carried on downwards and suddenly the narrow lane opened out into the wide space of the harbour. The sky expanded.

The derelict grain silo that Laurence had mentioned – a vast industrial relic, with its apron of concrete – sloped down to the shore. Seagulls wheeled and landed. Anita turned off her iPod to hear them. With her sense of smell sharpened, she caught a whiff of tar from the ropes and the marshy stench of decaying fish. She crossed in front of the silo and headed down a jetty, stepping over piles of rusty chains, past men fishing with lines, the day's necessities set out beside them: buckets, bait, flasks, tobacco, tin boxes of odds and ends.

The concrete arm stretched out and she wanted to continue; not with the desire to reach the far side – Georgia, was it? Her lungs inflated but there was no connection between her lungs and her mind – and no guard rails between her and the sea. To walk for ever seemed the answer but the jetty came to an end and she had no choice but to turn round and face the shore. The little town sprawled under the line of the hills; its buildings clustered at different levels on the crumbling cliffs. She picked out the minarets of a mosque and two church bell towers.

Back on land, Anita looked for somewhere to shop. The streets were quiet, disturbed only by the cries of gulls, or the rev of an engine. A woman, wearing the hijab, pushed a pram laden with bulging bags. A bare-headed little girl ran ahead of her across the slope of the harbour. Two old men stood on a corner for a chat and a smoke. Along the promenade, a retired couple, English or German, in their waxed jackets, strode out, legs moving in unison. They glanced at Anita, recognising a compatriot, or a fellow tourist type. She could count the number of people she saw. Holiday businesses were shut for the off season; the seaside bars not just locked but boxed up for the winter months; giant containers standing on the quayside like cargo waiting for a ship.

Anita came across a small general store, tucked away

in an alley. The interior was dark; the shelves mostly empty. A collection of neon-coloured fizzy drinks in two-litre bottles stood in crates on the floor. To one side was a small refrigerator that chugged loudly. A woman, half hidden behind the counter, was knitting a shawl in pink wool. Anita looked around. Sweets, batteries, 35mm camera film, yellow cheese, white cheese; the lack of choice reminded her of the British cost-of-living basket of decades ago.

She bought a few postcards, a packet of spaghetti, a tin of haricot beans, two tins of tomatoes, a bottle of wine and a bottle of water. The woman put her knitting down on the counter and carefully inserted the postcards into a fragile paper bag.

11

Sunday. Anita opened the windows on to the terrace. The apartment felt less alien. Her possessions were dotted about the place: cagoule, espadrilles, paperback books. They made patches of colour. She no longer noticed the sound of her own footsteps. She had mastered the kitchen tap. The bathroom smelled of coconut butter.

Anita sat out in the sun for a while and, as on the previous day, left The Hesperia in the late morning. Ignoring the car park, she walked around the perimeter of the development and discovered a track – a series of stepping stones across the sandy wasteland with the occasional sheet of hardboard placed to make up the shortfall. She followed this path through the dunes, taking her time on the uneven surfaces, and arrived at a rope strung between two wooden poles and an abandoned digger, tipped at a dangerous-looking angle with two wheels in a furrow. Beyond was the sea and the beginning – or, more accurately, the end – of the beach road that led to the resort. She saw the harbour in the distance – the outlines of the silo and the jetty.

She felt optimistic that she had found a route that avoided the main road.

When Anita arrived in the resort the harbour square was full of people. Boys were racing around, leaping over trailing cables, dodging round ice-cream vendors and crates of beer bottles. Van doors opened and balloons cascaded out, red, green and white, half floating, half tumbling.

A giant face was being pieced together on a makeshift hoarding. A fleshy slice of nose, a hairy nostril, one end of a grin with a suggestion of gold tooth. Each section was eased into place by a long-handled broom, then the ad stickers moved on. Men heaved blocks into position, assembling a temporary platform about six-foot high in the centre of the square. Lights were being rigged up and tested, insipid in the bright sun. An elderly man deposited his shopping bag on the bonnet of a car and lit a cigarette. A van splodged with crazy foam, and trailing with streamers, nudged the car's bumper and started hooting.

Anita made her way through the melee. She had no idea what was going on – politics or entertainment. It didn't seem to matter. The face might belong to the mayor, or to a crooner. She walked along the front and left the crowd behind. Booms from the harbour square grew faint.

*

Overnight, a sea fog developed. It was as if a glazier had come in the dark hours and replaced clear glass with opaque. Anita ran her fingers down the window, drawing lines that made no impression in the condensation. She unfastened the locks on the patio doors and stepped outside. The only visible objects were the set of matching garden chairs and table on the terrace. They stood out like items for sale on the white pages of a catalogue. She took in a few gulps of air. A wall of sea fog was just a few metres away, emptying itself of damp and cold. She wondered – since it was so silent – how fog could have woken her.

Something seemed to move within the whiteness. She caught a flutter from the corner of her eye. Although there was no hint of wind, a scattering of brown leaves was drifting into a pile on the paving slabs just beyond the terrace. Then a broom came behind them, then an arm, making short stabbing actions with the broom. Anita watched as a woman appeared. Her hair was dyed a deep aubergine shade and she wore a blue overall. It was Monday morning and work had resumed. The woman's movements were quick. Anita couldn't guess her age; anything between twenty-five and forty. Apart from Connor, she was the first person that Anita had seen on the premises.

The scene in front of her reversed itself; the leaves

pushed into nothingness, the broom, the woman. The swishing sound continued for a while, then stopped. Anita stepped back into the bedroom with her teeth chattering and shut the door. The cold took hold of her, exaggerating her shivers as her body shrank inside the T-shirt and pyjama bottoms. Her damp feet made prints of multiple toes on the tiles. There was no question of driving anywhere. She went back to bed, pulled the duvet up to her chin and closed her eyes.

When she woke again it was half past eleven. The fog was brighter, as though someone were beating sunshine into it.

The next day, the skies were clear. Anita made another attempt at driving and went in search of the bus station.

The sloping space, wide as a football pitch, was empty of buses. Five old men sat in a line, on a low concrete wall. A handful of abandoned flyers lifted lazily in the wind.

The timetable with its minute Cyrillic letters would have been unreadable even without the V-shaped tear down the centre but Anita pretended to examine it while the old men watched in silence, looking at her, she felt, as if she were an animal that had strayed down the hill; a sheep that gave the impression of wanting a bus. Eyes swivelled after her as she walked away. She continued upwards, climbing beyond corrugated iron roofs and tilting satellite dishes. Then the road ended. A burnt-out van marked the edge of the town. Anita took a sandy track across rugged ground, hoping that she might find at least one rural idyll and a photo opportunity.

When that path too petered out among chalky rocks, she stopped. Her plimsolls were full of stones. Turning back, she saw she had gained a view by climbing. From the high vantage point, she could see the sea, the light-house, the shoreline, dominated by the grain silo. She stood for a few minutes, watching vapour trails trace circles over Varna. She visualised belting towards Romania – inasmuch as a Fiat Uno could belt – knowing that reality showed a different kind of face from wishful thinking.

In her bag were two postcards with *Black Sea Greetings* splashed across the harbour view. One was to her parents, the other to Granny Randall. Having told them that she was going to a pretty fishing village once frequented by artists – not, as her mother had assumed, a holiday colony for worn-out Communists, or a tacky resort – she had taken up half the writing space apologising for the one-horse supermarket with limited stock. She thought of Veronica putting on the amber-framed reading glasses. Granny would be perplexed by the card. 'It's from Anita,' the carers would say. 'Your granddaughter. She's on holiday. Isn't that nice?' This wouldn't mean anything to Granny, though she knew Anita in the flesh.

On her phone were texts from friends, including a new one from Fran, that Anita hadn't replied to. Before setting off again down the hill, she sent back two-word responses: *And you*, *Me too*, *Oh good*. Anita switched off the phone.

At the moment of defeat, she always found herself back with herself; a girl – a woman – who didn't fully meet requirements. She remembered the feeling of the long holidays when she returned home from boarding school; the house empty; her parents, up in London, more than halfway through the working day. She saw the doors of her brothers' rooms, side by side. Strangely impersonal, almost like guest rooms, they housed a better class of being.

12

When Mark Mostyn announced that he was changing his degree course at Cambridge from law to economics Anita's parents involved themselves passionately. It was a subject they could both sink their teeth into and the discussion continued for weeks. At first, Anita thought that her father was in favour of the Bar and her mother of money, then she saw that it wasn't an argument, as such, but an analysis which they both came at, jointly and severally, from every direction. It assumed a shape, like a box with inner compartments, baroque decoration and a combination lock based on differential calculus. Mark remained absent throughout. He was sharing a house with friends in Cherry Hinton, outside Cambridge, and never communicated.

Anita was shocked by the continuing engagement her parents had with their children – or some of them – even when they had left home.

'What does it matter?' she asked Veronica.

'Of course it matters. It's his future,' her mother said.

'But that's not about *deciding*. It's about what happens to you.'

'That's a ludicrously fatalistic point of view. Decisions are hugely important,' Veronica said.

Eventually, the argument concerning jurisprudence versus economics, if it was mentioned at all, became some kind of dead matter, like last month's news, which they had all moved on from.

At the end of his second year at Cambridge, Mark travelled across the States with a group of friends. They hired a car and drove from coast to coast. There was no time for Hampshire that summer and Nick Halsey wasn't mentioned. Barney graduated with a first in mathematics. He had a job lined up with a firm of management consultants.

Anita was almost fifteen. She flitted about less. Her chosen colours were still bright but failed to match her mood. They were more like the sapphire blue jacket worn in the teeth of decay by an elderly woman. She had become more sedentary.

She continued to think about Nick. Boys she knew were pushy like her brothers, or nonentities. Mostly, they were too young; tame and unincendiary; powders in a toy chemistry set. They failed to figure in her wishful thinking. She was afraid of Nick Halsey but he was a secret comfort. She wanted the opportunity to look; to drink him in at her leisure.

Christmas came and went. Anita hated the empty days after the festivities and went to stay with Granny Randall. When she returned the guest bedroom door was shut.

'Who's here?' she asked Veronica.

'One of Mark's friends,' her mother said.

'Which friend?'

'I really don't know. They came in after we'd gone to bed.'

The friend slept late and appeared downstairs at about two in the afternoon.

'Hello, Anita. Did you have a good Christmas?' Nick Halsey said, spotting her as he walked across the hall in the direction of the kitchen.

'All right,' she said. 'Did you?'

He wore borrowed clothes, one of Mark's jumpers on top of his own and Mark's old school scarf wound round his neck. His eyes were bluer in winter.

He must have worked out how to operate the antiquated toaster because when she next saw him he was on the drawing-room sofa, propped against banks of cushions, reading a biography that Veronica had given Howard for Christmas. Beside him was a plate piled with toast, piccalilli and cold turkey. Anita noted Nick's woolly layers. Part of her lasciviously wished for summer and his shirt off – but she was no longer bold. She hid under layers herself.

'Cold in here, isn't it?' he said.

Anita nodded and wished for invisibility. The extra clothing and Nick's charming politeness made the situation just about doable.

She went to fetch a book and sat in the armchair that was furthest from the sofa. Partly concealed by the unlit Christmas tree – a seven-foot spruce that had shed a third of its needles – she wrapped herself in a rug. From time to time, she looked up. Nick's legs were crossed; an ankle rested on a knee, revealing the seams of his jeans where they met at the crotch. She raised her gaze, in case he caught her staring. His eyelids, as he read, formed perfect half-ovals; his expression was calm and focused. He might, she thought, have such a look when kissing.

Across the hall, in the yellow room, her mother was talking on the telephone. Through two closed doors, the insistent inflections of her voice penetrated. Even speaking normally, Veronica seemed to be protesting. Outside, along Gee's Lane, cars swished by in the rain. Anita tucked her feet into the folds of the loose covers of the armchair, curling her toes.

The girl on the summit of the load sat motionless, surrounded by tables and chairs with their legs upwards, backed by an oak settle, and ornamented in front by pots of geraniums, myrtles and cactuses, together with a caged canary – all probably from the windows of the house just vacated. There was a cat in a willow basket, from the partly-opened lid of which she gazed with half-closed eyes, and affectionately surveyed the small birds around.

The handsome girl waited for some time idly in her place, and the only sound heard in the stillness was the hopping of the canary up and down the perches of its prison.

Anita read page three of the first chapter of *Far from the Madding Crowd* very slowly, again and again. She got stuck in the wagon, between Emminster and Chalk-Newton, in winter sunshine.

Nick turned his pages over at regular intervals. Her mother kept talking.

Barney came in from a run. He breezed into the drawing room.

'Out,' he called to Viking, who had followed him in.

Barney's hair was whorled like crop circles. His cheeks glowed.

'Where's Mark, then?'

'Still asleep,' Nick replied.

'What are your plans for New Year's Eve?' Barney asked. 'I'm supposed to be going to this party in Maida Vale but there's a girl I'm trying to avoid. I might opt out.'

'Come with us, if you like,' Nick said casually.

He carried on reading. Normality was being able to turn pages. He wasn't bothered by any of the Mostyns. Anita perceived the imbalance.

Barney said he would make up the fire once he had towelled down the dog. But he continued to talk with his back to the fireplace, as rain from his clothing dripped on to the Chinese carpet. Nick eventually put the book down, open and jacket side up. There was a faint snap, as the spine gave way. Veronica wouldn't be pleased.

Anita crept from the room. She climbed the stairs to the top landing.

'Nick?' Mark croaked.

She pushed the door. The room was musky with the smell of fever. Mark half sat up and, seeing his sister, lay down again. She approached the bed.

'What's everyone doing?' Mark asked in a hoarse whisper.

Anita moved one of the curtains, in order to see him. 'Mum's on the telephone. I don't know where Dad is. Shall I open the curtains?'

'No. What about Barney? Where's Nick?'

His head glistened in the wedge of grey light that came

through the gap in the curtains. The duvet was coiled around him, stuck to him.

'Downstairs,' Anita said. 'Nick's reading. Barney's been out with Viking. He's just come in.'

'I'm ill,' Mark said.

'Shall I get you some paracetamol?' Anita peered at him.

'Has anyone mentioned New Year's Eve?' Mark struggled to release an arm and reached for the water glass. The whites of his eyes were as dull as mushroom skin.

Anita placed the glass in his hand. 'No one's said anything to me. It smells in here.'

'I'm ill,' he repeated. 'We're meant to be going to a party.'

'You might be better tomorrow,' she said, with a lack of conviction.

Mark grunted and turned to the wall. Anita waited. She expected he would ask her to convey some message to Nick but, breathing loudly through his mouth, he said nothing. Then he walloped over and settled on his other side. After a few moments, he gave a small gasp, a change of register, and sank into sleep.

New Year didn't affect Veronica and Howard. They were more desk diary than calendar people, guided by half-yearly figures and company year ends; these were the landmarks that joined time together for them. All the same, they had gone out. Dinner with the Bollards who lived about two miles outside Elvham. The Bollards had twins, Angus and Alaric. They played cello and viola in the National Youth Orchestra.

An hour after her parents' departure, with the rev of another engine and a scrunch of wheels on the front drive, Nick and Barney left for London in Nick's car.

The house was quiet; Viking asleep in the kitchen. Anita felt the outgoing year like a change of tides – but wondered whether the tide was coming in or going out. She already felt old. She sat in her room making lists that tended towards trivial – new stuff she wanted – but the words on the clean page of a notebook represented something greater than shopping: a transformation or psychic shift that would take her into a different part of the ocean.

She would have liked to be going to a party: dressing up, drinking, smoking one of the cigarettes that she kept out of sight in her tights drawer. Jessica Vale said she was having a party. In the last week of term, invitations on black paper, decorated with stars and skulls, had been passed round the class. J.V. rolled her eyes, acknowledging authorship, and claimed the event would be amazing. Anita hadn't heard again and presumed the party was a figment of J.V.'s imagination. In any case, how would she have got to Crowborough?

Anita felt sorry for herself, left alone with her brother. But there was a kind of purity in the occasion. She would see in the New Year on her own terms – Anita, not Mossy – and had already prepared a mirror. Old mirrors were best and she had taken down the shield-shaped one in the passage. Ideally she should blacken it with black paint. Now it was down from the wall, it seemed a fragile object. The wood that supported the frame had dried out and was cracked across in two places. She abandoned the paint idea, and relied on the age of the mirror; the blotches and freckles that were like spots of dark algae in a pond. She liked the word scry – midway between sky and cry, with sigh and scary hovering behind. She preferred it to prophesy. No one would believe her capable of that. In the back of her mind was the thought that she would have something to tell when the 'What did you do for New Year's Eve?' question came up. Her motives were as foxed as the glass. She didn't think magic would happen.

Fran was skiing with her family. So was Holly. Other girls would be at parties, though not as many as would claim to have been. None of them were Londoners. They would be stranded up country lanes or in suburban closes with a television. Vice would be limited and unsophisticated.

The magazine article said she should avoid catching her own reflection. She must look at the mirror from an angle and see into its depths, as though gazing into a lake.

Anita set the mirror on the table by the window. She had cleared it of pens and school books – also of Black Tulip nail polish which she had reapplied earlier. The room smelled of acetone.

A candle stood on the chest of drawers. Once lit, the flame kept its own neat circle of light some distance from the table. Another, on the top of the wardrobe, cast a full moon on the ceiling. Outside, the rain was easing. Anita heard drips in the gutter more clearly. She wondered how people – mediums and clairvoyants – cleared their heads of everyday matter. She supposed it was like school; all in the focus. Shut out the world and walk down a corridor towards a door marked 'Completed Coursework', or, in this case, 'Spirits'. She was easily distracted. Sidelong looks at the mirror showed nothing.

Colours will come and go, the magazine said. *With practice, you will see scried images like photographs developing, or even moving film.*

She anticipated a miracle time in the future when the real and the imagined would merge. Then thought of Veronica and Howard at the Bollards. Eight thirty for nine. The minor postponement to get them all comfortably through midnight, as though a more usual start time would trap them. She had noticed that her parents built in strategies to ward off panic.

'Granny's coming for lunch. I'll take her home straight after tea.'

Or, 'The Hadley-Woods have invited us to Joy's wedding but we can probably get out of the evening do.'

They set store by limits in order to free up time, though they didn't do much with their freedom. Her future would be different. Bathsheba Everdene, about to meet Gabriel Oak; a bachelor 'at the brightest period of masculine growth'. She was caught in transit, never arriving. For the moment, Anita forgot the caged canary.

The mirror was still inert at five minutes to twelve. By then, she was sleepy and had changed into her pyjamas. She picked up the candle from the chest of drawers. The flame shuddered at being transported. She set the candle down on the table and lay in bed, watching it. The curtains were unlikely to catch fire, being ancient velvet, greasy to the touch and heavy with interlining. Light lapped over the mirror, as the flame continued to flicker. The black freckling turned into fireflies. She was held by the beauty of light that wrinkled like water.

*

Waking on New Year's Day, Anita heard a bellow from downstairs. She got up and dragged open the curtains. As she ran her fingers down the window, the wavy lines in the condensation caught patches of moving colour.

Mark was wandering around the garden in his red checked pyjamas. She rubbed harder. Her brother held his head and, every few paces, banged it against invisible walls. Veronica, fully clothed, though without a coat, circled him, attempting to shield him from sleety drizzle with her green umbrella. Whenever she managed to grab his arm, he shook her off and continued to stumble about. Anita watched. She wondered how much of the year would be taken up with her mother pursuing Mark about the waterlogged lawn. She yawned and stepped back from the window.

Veronica played down the morning's events, pretending that it was quite normal to act Hamlet outside in pyjamas. She never colluded with Anita against the boys. An exasperated raise of the eyebrows would have made all the difference. But no.

Anita, determined to get to the bottom of it, kept asking questions as she ate her breakfast. Veronica said Mark wasn't himself, he was feverish. As the conversation was going nowhere, Anita went for shock tactics.

'Has he discovered he's HIV positive?' she asked.

Veronica was appalled and said that Mark had been disappointed not to go to the party in London.

'Upset about a party? How pathetic,' Anita said.

'I didn't say upset. I said "disappointed".'

'Oh, yeah. If he had had a gun, he'd have shot himself. I *saw* him, remember.'

'Anita, that's a horrible way to talk. "*Remember*", like that. It makes you sound even more gormless than you are.'

'Is he in love with Nick Halsey?' Anita asked.

There had been sightings of girls around Mark; young women who slicked their mean mouths with matte, caramel-coloured lipstick. They weren't the tame types whom Barney brought home. Veronica never doubted her sons' sexual preferences but Anita liked to needle her.

'Don't be ridiculous. He's not a silly girl. You're making something of nothing, as usual,' Veronica said.

'Well, he must be in love. Or he wouldn't be like this. You're in denial.'

It was Anita who was in love. She tested the words, scathing and unembarrassed. In the presence of the person least likely to empathise, she felt the grip of desire tighten.

'Stop talking in clichés. "In denial". Where do you get these dreadful phrases from?' Veronica left the room.

*

87

By the time Barney and Nick returned from London at around midday, Howard was boiling up the turkey carcass. The ground floor was full of rancid-smelling steam which found a way up through the house. Veronica sat, writing letters, in the yellow room. Mark was in bed.

'Turkey soup for lunch,' Howard announced, as Nick and Barney sloped in through the front door. It was his annual culinary effort and would be eaten with stale bread crisped up in the oven.

'Smells good,' Nick said politely.

'We crashed out in Fulham. Hope no one was worried. It was too late to ring. Did you and Mum have a good evening?' Barney said.

Anita, who was crouching on the stairs between the first and second floors, looked down at them through the banisters. Both boys were slightly swollen around the eyes but acting perky. Nick had looks that could take dissolution. The planes of his face had natural shadows. Barney, with the choirboy oval, had turned doughy.

Anita was in the middle of sketching, producing a staircase of Escher-like complexity. She admired Escher's tessellations and the way everything kept moving. She particularly liked the picture of people going upstairs and downstairs in an infinite loop. She found the endless rotations comforting – not a nightmare, as Fran thought – and wanted to draw something similar. She would add giant ants once the structure was in place. One of her New Year's resolutions was to draw more. Mr Larraway, the art teacher, said she spent too much time trying to be perfect. She should forget herself and be bolder.

'Tie back that hair you keep stroking and go for it!' Mr Larraway said.

She was incensed. As if she ever touched her hair, except to get it out of her eyes. As if she attempted perfection. 'Stroke' was a word that teachers should never use, even if they were having one and needed medical assistance. Fran said they should report Mr Larraway.

All the same, trying to get the fan-shaped turn in the steps, rubbing delicately with the rubber, Anita admitted that she was finicky. The subjects that appealed to her were labyrinthine. As a child, she used to construct palaces for worms.

When Nick and Barney came up to the first floor she shrank into the corner and covered her sketchbook with her forearm. They said 'Hello' and walked on past her, up to the top landing. Nick went into Mark's room and reappeared after a few moments.

'What's he saying?' muttered Barney.

'He's asleep. I didn't wake him,' said Nick.

Barney made some disingenuous noise of sympathy. 'Shall we go to the pub?' he said in a low voice.

'What about your dad's soup?'

'Worth missing. Trust me.'

They were already conspirators. Where had brotherly love gone? The famed togetherness of boys? Perhaps it had always been the case that visiting friends switched allegiance. Anita wasn't sure. Nick Halsey was fluid. He changed level, like water. She felt sorry for Mark.

Lunch was dismal. Life was elsewhere, more conspicuously than usual. Out at the Pheasant, upstairs in the sickroom. The three of them – Anita, Veronica and Howard – sat round the kitchen table in an atmosphere as vaporous as an old-fashioned washday, only smelling of poultry. Radio 4 was left on, argumentative in the background. Anita, wearing the purple leggings she had been given for Christmas, fished out hard red lentils with her spoon and placed them round the rim of her soup bowl. 'Loves me, loves me not . . .' There were questions she might have asked. Her parents wouldn't remember the seaside episode of the summer before last and, if reminded, would never make a connection. Are sibling scores ever settled, she wondered, or do they hang around as Destiny?

Mark kept to his room. He was ill, it was said, not sulking. Nick Halsey returned to London. Veronica, who hated home nursing, took up little trays. Anita heard her talking to her son, in a careful, palsy-walsy voice, as if she were a nurse dabbing around a gaping wound. Anita ventured into the room and spoke normally, showing it could be done. She wanted to be friendly.

'You're so loud, Netticles. Just bugger off, will you?' her brother said.

A day or so later, Mark came downstairs and then they all knew about it. His ability to dramatise went live, which didn't entirely work in pyjamas and dressing gown. He surrounded himself with an aura of pain. A thermometer hung from his lips like a cigarette holder, as he shuffled between rooms. He withdrew from Barney, whenever he appeared, making guttural noises of disgust and flapping him out of the way.

'He's barking,' Anita said to Veronica.

'No he isn't. Be more tolerant, Anita. He's always very nice to you.'

Anita boggled at that. 'Where have you been?'

Her mother lived in a closed world of sons and work and opinions. Keeping their weight revolving took intense organisation.

Anita resisted the force of the image Mark liked to project. If he had been a colour, it would have been gold, tarnished round the edges; if a drink, black coffee with a kick of poison. He was troubled in ways that she recognised. He wanted to be best. He wanted total allegiance. She could have been his ally but he never wanted to talk to her about things that mattered. She tried telling her mother he was flawed. In essence, she said, 'You may think he's perfect but I know he isn't.' Veronica wouldn't have any of it.

13

Builders down the road had begun excavating a basement. It was the third excavation in the terrace since January. A hill of earth and rubble had mounted in the narrow front garden and spilled on to the pavement. Drilling reverberated down the street. In the lulls, the noise of the Gunter Grove traffic resumed, like tinnitus.

Closing the front door behind her, Anita missed the soundproofed quiet of The Hesperia and the immaculate paintwork. The ceiling of the small hallway of the Chelsea house was half beige, half white, like a coffee/vanilla ice cream. A few years previously, someone had started redecorating and got halfway across. The two-tone look had grated for a while, then she had got used to it.

A scattering of post had landed on the mat in her absence: flyers, junk mail, envelopes with windows. The upstairs tenants had left shoe prints on them; the paper was mottled and criss-crossed with wavy grey lines. Anita stepped over the letters and the folded baby buggy and unlocked her second front door. This opened straight into the living room. Her flat smelled of home; the interior of a damp, long-used cupboard. Piles of unfiled papers drifted across the tops of books on the shelves; somewhere among them was an income tax return that should have been in by 31st October. She had been away for five days.

In the flat above, someone switched a television on. Anita heard the *Countdown* clock ticking. Then, when the time ran out, the jingle disappeared down a plughole. A child began to cry and the volume was lowered.

Anita wandered around in her coat. She switched on the central heating. Close to the Thames, the house soaked up moisture. The radiators took time to warm up; first they heated the furniture that was wedged against them; later, the air. She wheeled her bag over the dusty floorboards and into her bedroom and disgorged the contents on to the bed. She should never have bought a king-sized bed. Monstrous, at one end of the narrow room deemed fit for habitation by the builder who had done the conversion, it was accessible only by extreme contortions. She got in or out either by pressing herself against the cold wall, or by half crawling, half slithering towards the pillows, back again the same way. Now it was covered in clothes from the trip.

By the time the temperature in the flat had reached tepid, Anita could no longer be bothered to go out and shop for food. She poked around in the kitchen cupboard and found a selection of groceries similar to those in the one-horse supermarket by the harbour, though without the fluorescent-coloured drinks.

As she grabbed a handful of spaghetti and plunged it into bubbling water, her phone rang. She started, turning her head too abruptly, which set off the pain in her neck.

'How are the cottages?'

It was Fran in chirruping mood. She sounded close by.

'Mostly derelict,' Anita replied.

'Derelict sounds perfect. Keep shooting,' came back.

'Don't imagine I'm bombing around the countryside. The driving is really, really scary,' Anita said.

'You're not going meek on me, are you?' Fran was forthright. 'Meek' had been a term of abuse for her since schooldays.

Anita left the kitchen and walked from room to room, the phone pressed to her ear. She heard herself droning on about fog and potholed roads. The conversation wasn't a lie, as such; more a wrinkle in reality. She concealed her whereabouts but not her flakiness. This was something she could do; put herself down while missing out some crucial chunk of information. She wondered whether Fran could hear the Gunter Grove traffic.

'Find a man then, if it's that bad,' Fran came back. 'Is there one?'

Anita paused by the bedroom window and stared out through the silhouette of ivy. She described Connor, without mentioning the circumstances of meeting him. The sky behind the houses opposite was an uncanny, orangey, London colour.

'Seaside chavs so aren't telepathic. You'll simply have to ask him, darling. Fix up the insurance. Did you say he was the porter? He's probably dying to be asked,' Fran said.

Anita hadn't used those words to evoke Connor but something in the way she spoke of him had offered him up.

'Has Larry landed on you yet?' Fran asked.

'No, of course not, why would he?'

Fran laughed.

'He's in Montenegro, isn't he? Isn't he?' Anita repeated.

'Somewhere like that. He won't be able to resist dropping by,' Fran said.

'He said he wouldn't. Why would he?'

Fran laughed again. 'You're captive. He'll be wanting a piece of you.'

She went on to talk about their new nanny, Dahlia, who came from Estonia, and about Tim, her partner. They were all taking part in a run to raise money for the Heart Foundation. She asked Anita to sponsor her.

'Five pounds max,' Anita said and stopped listening as she drew the curtains, one-handed.

She thought about Laurence turning up – and Connor. Had she missed a solution to the driving problem? She got as far as wondering whether she could have swung a few expeditions into rural Dobrich, without having to spend too much additional time with the man with dyed hair and a tanned veneer. She felt anxious about what hadn't happened. She saw that he might have fastened on to her. Not a pulling in to the side and a lunge – she envisaged something more humdrum. Connor had been alone and possibly lonely. She had been alone – and, he might assume, lonely too. She imagined a creeping companionship. Knocks on the door to call for her, knocks on the door if he hadn't seen her for a day or two. She worried about using Connor and what he would have got in return for his chauffeuring. Her boundaries were gappy, like a badly maintained hedge. Surely they wouldn't have ended up shagging? For God's sake.

'Did you hear any of that?' Fran asked. 'Mossy, you are hopeless. I take the trouble to call you in Bulgaria, to lighten your life, and all you can say is "Mm." I do *know* you're not listening. Are you thinking of that porter person? Is he remotely fit?'

'No. He dyes his hair and wears a medallion.'

'Purely superficial.'

'Fran. I'm worried about Larry. Will he turn up?'

'It's only *Larry*. He just needs soothing. Stop being a

wuss.' Fran paused. 'You sound a bit weird. You'd tell me if anything was the matter, wouldn't you, Mossy? I don't mean the Larry crap. You promise you'd tell me . . .'

A few moments after the conversation with Fran ended, a text arrived from Veronica. The message was overlong and bizarre – a kind of miniature essay. Her mother gushed about Kendra's birthday dinner and asked about a life that wasn't happening; a parallel existence of 'hinterland', which Veronica hoped Anita was getting a feel for. Anita marvelled at 'hinterland' and wished, not for the first time, that her mother shared Howard's Luddite views on texting.

'Jesus,' she said and switched the phone to silent.

She opened a bottle of wine, poured a large glass and switched off the hob. Strands of spaghetti cooled in the pan. Anita sipped the wine and fished pieces of tomato out of the tin with a spoon. She ate absent-mindedly. Her phone, close by, was a familiar; capricious as a witch's cat. It watched her. She didn't reply to Veronica.

14

Wind blew in gusts from the west, bringing sheets of rain. In a lull, Anita forced herself out; across Battersea Bridge and into the park. Fountains in the Festival Garden were switched off for the winter. The Affordable Art Fair had been dismantled.

She kept to the avenues, semi-sheltered by the branches of trees. The leaves were mostly down, driven against walls and railings and moulded into soggy slopes. Lone joggers pounded the promenade, their hair slicked with rain. By the lake, the café glowed and steamed like a bread oven, the interior alight, its windows misty with condensation. Empty baby buggies lined up under the awning. They were left there by the nannies who gathered inside, drinking skinny lattes, holed up with their charges. Anita didn't stop for coffee.

All troops must break step when marching, the notice said on Albert Bridge. Hearing the hollow boom of vehicles as they rumbled passed her, she walked more lightly.

On the south side of the Thames, Anita continued on to Chelsea Harbour. In another downpour, she took refuge in one of the new developments; a self-contained world of durable flooring. Shops sold home furnishings and designer lighting. Apparently, no one needed sweets or a newspaper. Top-heavy security officers loitered, their thumbs in their belt loops. Men and women in suits walked about with clipboards. They were young and spooky, barely out of school, their faces smooth as waxworks.

Anita climbed to the top floor of one of the unoccupied blocks. She passed galleried landings and corridors; rows of identical apartment doors laminate-coated, with chrome numbers and spyholes like tiny glass eyes. Each floor was the same, only the light changed, becoming brighter as the ground receded. Paving slabs and empty flower tubs formed geometric patterns below. By cutting in and out, she obtained a panorama in segments: the London Heliport, Sands End gasometer, Lots Road Power Station. Everywhere, buildings were under construction.

At the top, Anita pushed open a door and, stepping out, found herself on an unofficial roof terrace that was shiny with puddles. A collection of satellite dishes rose beside her, looking, at close proximity, as if mobilised for war. She clung to the safety rail. From nine floors up, she could see the Thames looping in both directions. She stood for a few minutes, hanging on, as the rain blew in her face. Down the Black Sea coast at Sunny Beach and Golden Sands building had got out of hand. Whole villages of high-rise went up every day.

Men – it was usually men – left a pile of clothes on the shore and a car parked on a beach road. Then they went somewhere new; wore a hat, grew a beard, paid for plastic surgery. John Darwin, the phantom canoeist, had sailed to his death so that he and his wife could claim insurance and pension payments and start over in Panama. Another John – Stonehouse, an MP who was sunk in financial trouble – faked suicide on a beach in Miami and sugared off to Australia with his mistress.

Her time out was less dramatic; a trip to Bulgaria, summarily shortened. Perhaps everyone was doing it. 'Any holidays planned?' The secret knowledge that you would remain in Highbury or New Barnet. She had at least gone to the Black Sea for a few days. She had sent postcards to her parents and to Granny Randall; tangible proof.

It occurred to her, as she looked over Southwest London, that she had no need to say she was back.

Anita delved into the glove compartment of her car, pulled out an open packet of chewing gum, took out a piece of gum and placed it in her mouth. She beat slow rhythms on the steering wheel with the flat of her hands, imagining music.

'Day off?'

She looked up – a response that triggered the pain in her neck. In the last ten minutes, sitting pointlessly in her car, she had come to realise how frequently she turned it. A snatch of conversation, or a shout from one of the builders who were excavating the basement further along the terrace, started the habitual swivelling to look; an action now checked. She hadn't got herself down as a curtain twitcher and this bothered her as much as the pain. She was, it seemed, like a bird on a fence, forever on the lookout.

Through the open car window, she registered baggy trousers with a crease and a tired Viyella shirt that ballooned over a belt. The shirt rippled in the wind. She pushed the door, swung her legs out and walked round to the pavement.

Ivor was the only neighbour Anita knew by name. A fleshy, freckly man in his sixties, he had lived in the street for over twenty years and had an entire house to himself. He wore his usual capacious retro clothes. The Breton beret signalled colder weather.

'You noticed I wasn't going anywhere?' she said.

'I saw you get in,' Ivor said.

'And then nothing happened,' she said. 'I'm meant to

be working; driving around, taking photos of country cottages.'

As if a difficulty would lie down and wake up transformed – say, as a piece of cake. It woke refreshed, full of bounce, ready to be a difficulty all over again. She wrapped the blue cagoule tighter around herself.

'Sodding burrowers. Sodding Poles. Fuck the lot of them,' Ivor muttered.

He gazed down the road at the tent-like structure that concealed what had once been a front door. A builder emerged, tipped back his hard hat and lit a cigarette.

'What are you up to these days, Ivor?' Anita asked.

He turned to face her again; his expression milder. 'I've been doing some trading on the Internet – Falklands War memorabilia.'

'Sounds fun,' she said.

'It passes the time. I don't make any money out of it.' Ivor paused. 'You haven't turned into an *estate agent*, have you?'

He whistled and his dog, Lily, who had been sniffing a pile of sand left by the builders, rushed forward and licked Anita's ankle. She was a retired greyhound with a long, lilac-coloured tongue.

Anita bent to stroke her. 'No, this is just a project for a friend.'

'Good. I wouldn't want to think of you working for

those toerags. This bloody country is obsessed with property. They buy it *and* they talk about it. People think because I'm white and speak the Queen's English that I'm as interested as they are. Well, I'm not. I suppose we're in for another day of incessant racket while our neighbours dig themselves the Hellhole. What will they put in it? A home cinema, a staff toilet? Christ, I hate nowadays.'

'I'm meant to be taking photos of country properties that are totally undone up. Ideally they would be witchy and tumbledown. Maybe belonging to very old people. Only I haven't found any yet. Do you know of anywhere, Ivor?' Anita said.

'Seldom leave London these days. If it weren't for Lily I wouldn't ever get out of the house.' Ivor mused on his indolence. Then he came out of his reverie. 'Well, it's been good to catch up. Cheerio.'

He raised a hand and wandered off down the road in the direction of Brompton Cemetery, his habitual dog-walking destination. Lily bounded ahead of him in elegant undulations. The sky was a business-like grey without sparkle.

Anita locked the car. Her inability to drive oppressed her. She wondered what else was in store.

Indoors again, she went online and took down the telephone numbers of the best people for systematic desensitisation. She made another list for cognitive behavioural therapists. She downloaded a DVD that taught progressive muscle relaxation. The chirpy man in an open-necked shirt talked of 'gradually exposing yourself to the phobic object', which Anita found hilarious until she remembered that the phobic object was the driving seat of a car. After a while, she tired of the semi-medical approach, made herself some tea and emptied the washing machine.

Chelsea didn't offer much in the way of Bulgarian architecture. What had her mother thought of as typical? Whitewash, dovecotes, overhanging roofs. She needed a lodge, a cottage ornée; somewhere quirky. She wondered, vaguely, about the outer zones on the Transport for London map, since driving was out of the question. She could alter the images, blacken them and add the odd downpipe.

At some stage, she would style out her malfunctioning, make a joke of it.

15

Gavin Peace had admitted to a mother in Perthshire and a sister in East Grinstead. His father, he had said, was 'somewhere in the southern hemisphere'.

'Does your sister see your mother?' Anita had wanted to know.

'Pass,' Gav had replied.

His pronouncements on indoctrination and the social collective were impassioned and unrelated to everyday life. Gav never gave examples. Anita assumed this was a male thing. Her brothers could orate. If she pushed Gav too far with questions about his relatives, he left the room or changed the subject.

Anita kept her distance from her own family. The dutiful suppers came later. Although Mark and Barney were both in London, Anita rarely saw them. News was filtered through Veronica. Her mother, who rang up from time to time, talked at length but Anita sensed that she too lacked information. Veronica wasn't making a selection from a pool of knowledge; she passed on, verbatim, the contents of a longed-for telephone call. Her sons were successful, made money, mixed with other similar people, some of whom, unsurprisingly, turned out to have been at school with them. This made Veronica happy, even though much was concealed from her.

'Oh hello, Mrs Mostyn. Anita's right here.' Gav waved the handset away from his face. 'Yours, Anita.'

She was a free spirit – free as Gav – yet, hearing her mother's voice, Anita felt tugged by a current towards a stretch of English mainland she had thought she had left behind. For the duration of the call, she was in two places and queasy in both.

'What was that about?' Gav asked afterwards.

'Nothing, really. Nothing worth repeating. She likes to talk.'

Sometimes, Anita agreed to participate in the arcane postal system devised by the Randalls to cause maximum hassle. Granny and Veronica had a long-held prejudice against queuing at the post office. They used Royal Mail for letters but anything bigger, or that needed weighing, was dispatched by a mazy system that involved car journeys and waiting for someone to visit, say, Edinburgh.

Around the time of her twenty-fourth birthday, Anita was told that a parcel from Granny had arrived and was sitting on the dining-room table in the Eccleston Mews house. On a free afternoon, she went to collect it.

Cut off from traffic, the mews was quiet – and, with the sun shining, invited a deck-chair or two, though, as far as Anita knew, no one ever made use of the space. Lacking ground-floor windows, the facades were shuttered and expressionless. Anita had never once seen neighbours. Someone's cleaner was letting herself out of a house. She held a black plastic bag tied with a knot at the top which she deposited in a wheelie bin.

Anita's key stalled – the mortise lock wasn't engaged. Howard must have been the last out, she thought. He was the absent-minded one. She inserted the Yale and opened the black painted door. As it closed behind her, she heard the hum of the fridge from the kitchen. The place was shut in on itself; the air stale. Anita stepped over envelopes that were lying on the mat and went through to the dining room. She switched on the overhead light. The curtains were drawn over the garage doors, as usual. One end of the table was piled with box files and papers, the other kept clear for eating. There were the two used, rolled napkins in unmatching silver rings, the pepper grinder and the salt cellar, a half-empty bottle of wine, stoppered with a cork – and Granny's parcel, wrapped in gold foil left over from Christmas.

The gloom of the place overwhelmed her. Anita picked up the package quickly. She felt like an intruder who has spotted something not meant to be seen; daily arrangements, which, in the inhabitants' absence, were tinged with pathos. Her parents were too busy – too attached to themselves – to steal up on their life, unawares. They were middle-aged and married and immersed themselves in work. They wouldn't know that they left tell-tale signs of mortality and a smell of boiled potatoes. Anita blamed them for their oversight – but wondered whether the flower seller in Belgrave Square would be on his pitch outside the Spanish Embassy. She would go and see. If not flowers, she would, at least, leave a note. She switched off the light.

'Mother?'

Anita dropped the package. 'For God's sake, Mark. You nearly gave me a heart attack.'

'Netticles. It's you. What are you doing here?' Her brother's head appeared over the top of the drawing-room sofa.

'What are *you* doing here? Why didn't you say anything when I came in?'

'Sorry.' Mark slid down again.

Anita retrieved the parcel and walked round the furniture into the middle of the room. Mark was lying down; his head balanced on one of the armrests, his knees bent. He wore an expensive-looking suit, a striped shirt with a loosened tie at the neck, and a pair of red socks.

'Is that a present for me?' he asked.

'No. It's not your birthday,' Anita replied.

'Well, it's not yours yet, is it?' Mark manoeuvred himself until he was sitting upright with his feet on the floor. 'Sixteenth June is imprinted on my mind. Dad taught us how to play gin rummy the day you were born.'

'So you always say. Granny's ahead of herself, but she's allowed to be.' Anita remembered the dining-room table. 'How are Mum and Dad?'

'They seem all right. I haven't seen much of them. They're out a lot. In answer to your first question: I'm camping here for a week or so. I sold East Acton and I'm buying Hammersmith.' His expression lacked trust although she was his sister. The eyes he had once used to intimidate – slightly bloodshot, she noticed – failed to meet hers. 'I don't *live* here, Netta. I haven't slept here more than once. Some of my stuff's here.'

'Just afternoon kips on the sofa, then?' she said. 'Seems like an easy life. Your boss doesn't mind? Maybe you *are* the boss.'

'I work bloody hard. They're lucky to have me. I had rather a heavy lunch, as it happens.' Mark rubbed the back of his head. 'If you were feeling kind, you could make me a cup of coffee.'

It was as though he were on the other side of a road, separated from Anita by moving traffic. He might catch sight of her and give her a wave but he never crossed over.

Anita went into the kitchen. She returned with a mug and a glass of water and, a few minutes later, with a pot of coffee.

'Angel. Thank you,' Mark said. 'Aren't you having any?'

'No. I've got to get back. I'm working this evening.'

Anita was a waitress for a catering company. She handed round canapés and topped up glasses. It was a job she fell back on when daytime work dried up. She wore black and tied her hair in a knot.

Mark failed to ask the banal question. She might have been in the chorus of a musical by Andrew Lloyd Webber – or an escort. He wasn't interested.

'I'll see myself out,' she said, though he hadn't budged.

She blew him a kiss, as she opened the front door. 'Let me know when you move to Hammersmith.'

'Of course I will, Netticles. You must come round. We'll walk by the Thames and watch cormorants.'

16

The road outside Cheshunt Station was full of puddles that reflected a mottled sky. Anita, with her camera in her bag, set off towards the Lea Valley in search of Bulgarian houses. Cars passed frequently. In a nearby field, a horse grazed between brambles. It looked up with a long, serious face as Anita passed, then went back to munching. The chance of coming across a house that would look at home in Dobrich was small but maybe, between trees, in the right sort of light . . . Anita felt hopeful.

At the River Lea, she turned northwards along the towpath. Two boys with shaved heads sat side by side, fishing. Further on, a short, plump man in a tracksuit pushed one leg against a post, stretching his hamstrings. She continued. The water lapped beside her.

She had once seen a film about a Japanese businessman who was made redundant but omitted to tell his wife. He left for work in the morning, as usual, and walked purposefully around the city park. At lunchtime, he gobbled his snack. He set his mobile to ring and answered non-existent calls. Men in suits strolled by, also on their mobiles. One of them turned out to be in the same position as the former manager, dressed for employment, with nowhere to go.

Anita had thought at the time that there was something peculiarly Japanese in this behaviour but her pretence was similar. Sidestepping normal life opened up an odd landscape, familiar but different, like having to take the replacement bus instead of the train. She wondered whether she was still herself when family and friends imagined her elsewhere. They continued to communicate. The oddness of this troubled her but, nearly a week after her return from the Black Sea, she hadn't admitted she was back. Texts and emails were like random mailshots, or cold calls from India. She expunged them without replying. If she sent news from Dobrich there would be no end to the fakery. She couldn't take on a bantering, gap-year persona. No pictures of her downing tequila shots under a full moon. No pictures at all. Sometimes she remembered Laurence's apartment and felt nostalgia for the place she hadn't much enjoyed; the empty beach, the strange calm of The Hesperia.

Having been cooped up, in and around the Chelsea flat, Anita felt suddenly free and wondered why she hadn't got out before. A bicycle sped past, bell jangling. Anita stepped aside and resumed walking. Her thoughts were looser than when she was stuck indoors; shaken out like beads on slack elastic. On a houseboat, a woman was cleaning windows. The river moved on, never completed. Every liquid drop merged with another and caught a different aspect of light as it flowed.

Anita had done the same walk with Miles Greener. They had set off from Stoke Newington. The shared house where he lived had looked normal from the street but inside was hazardous. 'Just watch the . . .' 'You need to . . .' The upstairs windows wouldn't open; his bedroom smelled of toothpaste and socks. In the corner was a basin, veined with dark cracks. She had been glad then, too, to get out into the air – though later they climbed over a fence and broke into a shed in someone's riverside garden. She remembered the scent of new pinewood and the constant lapping of water. People passed on the towpath, metres away, unaware of them and what they were doing. There was something exciting about the footsteps, the louder-than-life talking and laughing just the other side of the thin wooden walls, while they suppressed their giggles and scrabbled with clothing. They were hungry, having skipped breakfast, and had eventually found a pub that warmed up steak pies in a microwave. Afterwards, they went back into London by bus from Waltham Abbey. They waited an hour, and finally one rolled into view; its top deck brushed the leaves of overhanging trees.

On a straight stretch of the River Lea, Anita came across a lock. Two sets of gates with their winding gear were separated by a deep, man-made chamber that was mysteriously part of the river. At first, Anita failed to notice the lock-keeper's cottage. Uncut grass met the walls, fringing the base of the building. Paths and boundaries had sunk in a green tide. Bricks, windows and chimney stacks emerged between a weave of saplings like a repeat pattern in a carpet. The upper storey overhung the lower, and the tiled roof overhung them both, making double layers of shadow. To one side was a dilapidated garage, its roof chequered by missing slates. A young sycamore had grown through one of the spaces. Branches shot out between rafters.

She paused on the riverbank. The interior would be like the bottom of a well. Light the colour of moss would filter through the windows. For a moment, she fantasised about living there. It was a glimpse of a life that appealed to her, a form of playing house; somewhere secluded and miniature that could contain and hide her. The trees would encroach. Miles had been happy to be holed up in a stranger's shed with her. Her present reverie was a mix of fairy stories – and mostly bogus.

Anita hesitated. She scrabbled about in her bag for her camera, stirring up a jumble of stuff; her phone, make-up kit, a clutch of tissues, a scarf in a ball. A whiff of cosmetics escaped, as if some immaterial part of her were contained there. She located the camera and snapped shots in rapid succession. The electronic clicks sounded flat in the still air.

If the trigger to purchase a retreat in rural Bulgaria was, in fact, a picture of a cottage in the outer suburbs of London, who was to mind? Anita recalled the mock-up views of The Hesperia: the blue pool full of water, the hedges waist-high. The dreamer was already trawling through property web brochures, innately dissatisfied about something. Dissatisfaction was the transgression – the beam in the eye – the rest was commerce. The final stage was parting with money, paying lawyers, employing builders, kitting a place out. She clung to the thought that the Illyrian coast where Gwyneth Paltrow was washed up at the end of *Shakespeare in Love* had been Holkham beach in Norfolk. It was a question of imagination and keeping an open mind.

Her next photo shoot that day involved farm build-ings. Anita's spirits lifted at the sight of rust, mud, puddles of oily water, rags of fabric caught on barbed wire, wheelless vehicles and their near relation, the pile of worn tyres. A caravan was parked on an area of concrete and next to it an old van with curtains at the windows. On the plus side, from a bourgeois standpoint, were patches of potato cultivation among dead sunflower stalks, a line

116

of blue jeans pegged out to dry and a collection of satellite dishes that mushroomed from ramshackle roofs. A white goat grazed in a charred circle of grass. She felt nervous hanging around other people's territory and nearly dropped the camera when a boy came up behind her. He was about eight years old; overweight and dressed in all-in-one waterproofs.

'You from the Academy?' He was out of breath, as though he had hurried to catch up with her.

'No, I'm not,' Anita said. 'Is this where you live? Is it OK if I take a few photos?'

'Of me?' he asked, astonished and a little bit wistful. His head was as round as a ball.

'Would you like me to? I can,' she replied.

'No, 's OK. You go ahead.'

'It's just the farm buildings I wanted – for an art project.'

The boy shrugged his shoulders. ''S OK.'

He loitered around her, kicking stones, while she fiddled with the camera – and waved when she left.

By late afternoon, Anita had amassed a collection of photographs. Scrolling through the miniature pictures, on the train back to Liverpool Street, she doubted the properties would pass as Balkan. She couldn't send them to Laurence, she decided. The idea of counterfeiting scenes of Dobrich was a joke.

A fast train tore past with a whoosh that sucked air from the carriage. With its vanishing, the view resumed: houses, roads, a recreation ground where a child swung to and fro at a stately pace, pushed by his mother.

At Southbury Station, a crowd of schoolboys in green blazers swarmed along the platform and on to the train. One person remained; a young man, who half rose from a bench, as if going to board, then thought better of it and slumped back down again. He took a swig from a hip flask. He was in his late twenties and wearing a suit.

The woman who sat opposite Anita looked up. She stared at Anita, then at the upside-down screen of the camera that had slipped to the floor. When Anita bent to retrieve the camera the woman went back to texting. Further down the carriage, the schoolboys brawled and shouted obscenities.

17

The following morning, Nick Halsey rang. Anita was out in the back garden, fishing blackened, wet leaves out of the kitchen drain. The phone slithered around in her yellow rubber gloves. It was odd to hear Nick's voice; nice too. 'Aren't you back yet, Anita? We miss you,' he said.

He used to mention missing in the gaps between their assignations. The words were always said breezily – though not in the plural. He had been breezy throughout their brief affair, though sometimes he groaned about his own stupidity in loving her and then Anita found herself trying to cheer him up, as though she were a third party who happened to have strayed into bed with them and joined the conversation.

'How's Emma?' Anita struggled with the rubber gloves that were slippery with black slime. She tried to keep her voice upbeat.

'Good,' he said, 'though she gets a lot of backache. The baby's pressing on a nerve.'

Anita sympathised. She kept shaking her free hand, trying to release her fingers from the glove.

Nick said he was in Paris attending a meeting.

'I can hear the traffic. Paris hooting,' she said.

'What's it like there?' he asked her.

'Hang on,' she said.

Placing the phone on the ground, she pulled off both gloves. Nick's voice carried on, tinny in the speaker.

She put the phone back to her ear. 'Sorry,' she said.

The gloves lay half inside out; yellow and white, streaked with greenish-black tracks.

'Anita, what's going on? You went away,' Nick said.

'It was a pigeon,' she said. 'It landed on the duvet.'

'God! It just flew in?'

'No, the duvet's outside, hanging over the hedge. I'm outside too, on the terrace.'

'This is too complicated for me,' Nick said.

'Everything here has a funny smell. Sort of chemical. I suppose it's because the building's brand new. I have to air stuff.'

She described The Hesperia, trying to be amusing. She mentioned the empty swimming pool, the long corridors, the woman with aubergine-coloured hair. All the while, she stared at her small patch of lawn that was more mud than green. The sparse grass lay every which way. Around the perimeter were three different types of fence; the responsibility of three separate and adjacent owners. Anita's, to the left, was rotten in places, held together by ivy; straight ahead was a weave of blond wood; to the right were sturdy panels topped by trellis. The trellis neighbours had recently had their garden made over into a bower of pleached hornbeam.

'It doesn't sound great,' Nick responded. 'Are you sure you're all right?'

'I'm good. It's not a fair contest, Nick; Avenue de l'Opéra, or wherever you are, and a Black Sea apartment development out of season.'

He asked her about the photography.

'Only a few cottages, so far. It's not easy getting about here. The roads are dire.' Her usual refrain; she was getting sick of it.

'So where did you go yesterday?' he asked.

'I found a cottage in the middle of a forest.'

'I hate to think of you in these isolated places. Should you be doing this on your own?' Nick said.

'Oh don't worry. There was no one there. A pair of old trousers. With braces. They were hanging over the back of a chair.'

'You went inside? Bloody hell. He could have come back at any time,' Nick said.

'He would have been wearing a spare pair of trousers.' Anita found it hard to concentrate, aware of a faint hissing that was growing louder. She kept on talking.

Suddenly, the next-door garden came alive in explosive

121

splutters. Anita stepped back. A spray of water cascaded over her, smelling like salad left too long in a plastic bag.

She kept saying she was sorry.

'What's happening now?' Nick asked.

'The irrigation's started up. God knows why at this time of the year.'

'What kind of irrigation? Where are you, Anita?'

'There's a hedge round the terrace here. Each apartment has its own patio thingy – and the swimming pool's in the middle. Only it's empty. Are there EU rules about grey water? Or can it come from anywhere?' she asked.

'Anita, I haven't called to discuss the disposal of Bulgarian sludge. Go and rescue your bedding, for heaven's sake.'

'Bedding? Oh, the duvet.' She wondered why he *had* called.

'It's time you came home. When are you coming home?' he asked. 'It's your brother's wedding, isn't it?'

She kicked the doorstep.

'Anita?'

She told him, truthfully, she hadn't decided when she would return.

'Don't go too far off-piste,' Nick warned. 'I'm worried about you now. I was slightly worried and now I'm really worried. Come back soon.'

She sent her love to Emma. They said goodbye. The

flurry of communication over, Anita was alone with the sputter of water and the hum of traffic. After a few more seconds, the neighbours' watering system settled into more regular spurts. Narrow rivulets of water inched under the fence.

Anita went back indoors and slammed the door. She sat down at the kitchen table, put her head in her hands and sobbed. Although she had been on her guard and had tried to sound cheerful, she had ruined the conversation. She had talked readily, far too readily; like an elderly person seldom visited. Impressions, real and imagined, had tumbled out. A pigeon, for God's sake. Where had that come from? Nick Halsey had a knack of uncovering her. She could say nothing – or something plainly false – and reveal herself. Even on the telephone, she seemed to show her face to him.

She should never have mentioned a forest. The Viennese doctor in the sky would have picked up on that. 'Ah so, Miss Mostyn. We know you better than you know yourself, isn't it?' But Nick, had he noticed? In the game of associations, he would follow a different path. *She* had been in a travelling trance that afternoon, looking at the scenery passing, as though watching an undemanding film, not expecting what happened next, not expecting anything. Nick had left the main road and turned on to a track across Ashdown Forest. As they drove along, he remarked that the forest was mostly heathland, not forest at all, which struck her as plausible, things often being different from what they were called. Nevertheless they were heading towards trees.

The wood, when they reached it, had the charmed force of the real. It was odd how the film just stopped. She was caught unawares. Damp air washed into the car, and silence, sharpened by odd rustlings, overpowered the sound of the engine that chugged at low speed. She glanced at Nick – the creases in the sleeves of his shirt. He was leaning forward, concentrating on the ground under the wheels, his face set, as if engaged on a necessary task. Driving in and out of slivers of sun, they were dazzled. Nick put the visors down but the effect was still like an on/off switch. He drove off the track into a clearing, brushing through bracken. The world was as clear as glass.

Looking back, she wasn't sure when the clarity had ended – whether suddenly, with an edge, or slowly merging into the grey of normal life – or if it had ended at all. Sometimes colours were far too bright.

It was easier to remember an onset. Like a child who turns a mirror over and finds not the reality expected, but an opaque surface, she carried on turning the memory over and over to try to make sense of it. She could never decide between Nick's innocence and his brazenness. He seemed to want to keep in touch and she wondered whether that was from guilt. He had taken advantage of her. Or maybe he hadn't. Taking advantage was an old-fashioned concept. Jesus. Give over thinking about it.

Anita sniffed and rubbed her eyes with her sleeve. She went over to the sink and rinsed her face with water from the tap. The sink was still blocked; the rubber gloves lay outside in the garden.

18

Though stagnation in the property market made him feel a little bit dead, autumn suited Laurence Beament. It was his time of year. Early darkness, the formality of winter clothes, the buzz of hyperactivity. Summer brought people on to the streets, but not anyone Laurence knew. In the last quarter of the year, London produced old acquaintances at random. Sometimes they recognised him, sometimes they spent a few moments wondering who the hell he was, but he didn't mind; just seeing someone he recognised in a theatre crush bar, getting out of a taxi, or walking, head down in the rain over Holborn Viaduct, gave him a feeling of being at home in the world.

He had returned from Montenegro discouraged by the financial downturn. He was going for a wait-and-see policy over foreign investments – *mer et montagne* – on the margins of the former Soviet bloc. Current projects were on hold. On the whole, he considered himself better placed than the friends who had bought buy-to-let, canal-side apartments in the West Midlands.

Although things were a touch rocky money-wise, he

kept serene. He thought of Mossy in his apartment in The Hesperia and had an inkling that he had done a good deed. The word 'rescue' came to mind – he felt his action was somewhere on that spectrum.

He had detected, he thought, a flicker of interest from her at the Chelsea dinner. He wasn't someone who was bombarded by sexual signals. When they happened, he recognised them. Once or twice, he had to admit, he had overinterpreted a flicker.

Laurence was in no hurry to disturb Mossy. He believed that he might scare her away with attention. Sometimes, in order to strike a deal, it was necessary to throw everything into the process and negotiate into the small hours; at others, one had to bide one's time. He was capable of both approaches, in love and business; possessing, he believed, a tigerish and a pastoral side.

Mossy had been in Bulgaria for nearly two weeks but he still hadn't heard from her, or been in touch since her arrival – though he was under pressure from Fran so to do. Fran seldom contacted him, so her sudden attention both gratified and needled him.

'You give her some futile assignment in the back of beyond and *retreat*. She'll be lonely. She'll go nuts. I mean, are you managing this project, or not? Larry, you are just so *limp*.'

He had endured several of these blastings on the phone

and had temporised. Then, just as he was getting slightly twitchy himself about Mossy's silence, he ran into Fran in Jermyn Street, late one afternoon.

'Buying for your menfolk?' Laurence asked, having kissed her cold cheeks. 'Don't let me hold you up.'

Fran suggested tea.

'Christmas always takes me by surprise. How clever of you to be organised,' he said, ignoring the suggestion.

'Larry. You're absurd. It's far too early. Only November. These are for me.' She waved carrier bags bearing the names of familiar gentlemen's outfitters.

'I'd no idea. Have you come out, Fran? You always look so feminine.'

'Larry, Jermyn Street sells women's clothes nowadays. Work clothes.'

'How ghastly.'

She was wearing a tailored coat, unbuttoned, and underneath he made out a white shirt and sober skirt that suggested she was taking her finals for the umpteenth time. Her long hair, exuberantly wavy, bounced like a chatelaine's in a costume drama bed scene. Subfusc often came with an erotic charge. She seized his arm, in a manner that was entirely womanly, and was steering him away from the beautiful lighted windows full of striped shirts and cheerful ties.

'But, darling, I don't *want* tea.' Laurence pulled away and raised a hand in farewell. 'Must dash. I need new socks.'

Fran grabbed him by the sleeve of his overcoat before he could escape. 'I'll buy you a pack tomorrow and send them to you. Are you large or extra large?'

'Fran, I'm a mere nine and a half. Please don't draw any false conclusions. The penis/foot thing is a myth.'

'Oh, Larry. Honestly.'

She tugged him along the street, past the contented-looking gents who chug between St James's Street and Piccadilly, and whirled him through a revolving door. He found himself in a crowded interior, stuffy with cooked-cheese smells. Tourists toyed with plates of early supper, crusted with reheating. In front of a counter of elaborate gateaux, two small Italian boys fought with teaspoons.

Fran propelled Laurence towards a walnut-veneered table that was smeared with chocolatey rings and morsels of slimy macaroni. She stowed her bags away under one of the chairs. Laurence refused to sit down. Fran protested that she needed tea. Laurence huffed and puffed. He acted like a grumpy, elderly man. People began to look at them.

Fran gave in and stood up. Laurence retrieved the bags and badgered her out. They were back in damp London air and this time Laurence did the steering, placing his gloved hand in the small of Fran's back. They wove in and out of caged roadworks, stepping on and off the pavement. Taxi drivers hooted at them. Eventually, in a side street, they went down cellar steps and into a bar. Here were bulky pillars and pools of darkness; barmen drawing corks. Laurence breathed in the soothing smell of booze.

They found a quiet corner. Laurence went to buy drinks. Fran, divested of the coat, relaxed. Her white shirt and pearls gleamed from the shadow of a pillar. The front page of an old evening paper, jammed down behind the bench seat, showed a picture of bank employees clearing their desks. Boxes, pot plants, golf clubs, all ceremoniously carried out.

'Turn it over, Larry. I don't want to know,' Fran said. 'It will be us next. Let's talk about something nice.'

She had had lunch with Jemima. Her photographs of the Himalayan trek were hilarious. Inevitably, Fran got on to the subject of Mossy. Laurence listened and smoothed back his hair.

'I got the weirdest reply to a text. "Me too", it said. That was all. It made absolutely no sense. That bloody mother of hers and the wedding plans for the worshipped son and the spoiled American woman. They both need their bottoms smacked, in my opinion.' Fran took a gulp of wine. 'You know it was just before Barney's first wedding that her other brother had the accident?'

'Yes.' Laurence paused. 'I heard about it at the time – must have been from Gareth Hyssop. He knew Mark Mostyn. I didn't. Neither of her brothers. I've never met Mossy's family. What are they like?'

'Haven't you? Dad's a sweetie, but petticoat-governed. "Don't go to the wedding," I told her when she moaned about it. Your Bulgarian trip was a godsend, Larry. "Stay for months," I said. "No, bad idea, because then I won't see you." I adore Mossy. She's my *oldest* friend, you know. But honestly, Larry, I'm worried. She's gone quiet. And normally she communicates. She sounded different when I called her. She's too isolated. There's no one there apart from the porter person.' Fran widened her eyes.

'Who?' Laurence asked. 'Who are you talking about? The Hesperia doesn't have a porter.'

'Hesperia? What a terrible name. You must get it changed, Larry. It sounds like some kind of disease. No, Mossy definitely mentioned someone. Connor, I think he was called.'

'Arguably, a porter might be a good idea,' Laurence said.

'Well, whoever. There is some man there.'

Laurence pondered. He stroked his hair. Fran had rattled him but he wasn't going to admit to it. Preferring to deal with the matter in his own time, he decided to lie. He allowed Fran to run on before saying, casually, that Mossy had sent him some photos.

131

'Are they on your phone? Let's have a look,' Fran said.

He put his hand to his jacket pocket, protectively.

'Larry, for God's sake, why didn't you say so straight away?'

He gave an enigmatic smile. 'The pics are excellent. Hansel and Gretelish.'

'Let's see. They sound twee,' Fran said, leaning towards him.

Laurence moved out of reach. He kept his hand on his heart. 'A socialist realist production,' he said. 'Rooted in the landscape and unmucked about. She has an eye. The clients will love them.'

'Idyllic. How many have you got?' she asked.

'A goodly number.'

Fran gave him a sidelong glance. 'Clients?'

'Interest has been shown.' Laurence sipped his vodka in the shadow of the corner.

19

The Hertfordshire excursion wasn't repeated. Anita stayed in and around Chelsea, keeping to the off-streets. Clothes shopping and the King's Road were out of bounds. She might bump into someone. In any case, she had no money.

For several mornings in a row, she went back to bed with a cup of tea and watched television: real-life confessions, the news and the weather, financial gloom, bombings, British soldiers dying in faraway places, cliffhanger endings, slip-sliding misery, property makeovers and wardrobe transformations. When sports commentators barked and bellowed she turned off the sound, leaving players careering in silence over the pitch. On a bad television day, she resembled Granny Randall whose sense of reality ebbed and flowed.

She had lived like this before – but patchily. She didn't want to remember the period when she had kept to her bed for weeks. It seemed as though dullness seeped from her life into her face – and her voice. Voice was beyond control. She knew that from other people. Without drama training – which she wished she had had – vocal sound was a link to the parts of the mind that she hoped to keep hidden.

She saw how retirement might go – a sameness day on day. But she wasn't retired and the hours went slowly. She felt under pressure, from her mother, from anyone who sent a text or an email. The random messages based on misconception made her feel alone and disconnected. Was this how spies and bigamists lived? Her situation was without glamour.

Veronica no longer enquired about hinterland. She was fussing about Anita's return flight from Varna, insisting that she book one, insisting on knowing the date.

'Anita, you haven't replied to any of my texts. Is everything all right? We've been worried about you.' Veronica spoke loudly, as if distrusting the signal.

Anita aimed the remote and turned off the sound on the television. She was lying in bed under rugs, at eleven in the morning, watching a programme on living statues. The current one, sprayed silver, was dressed in doublet and hose. Tourists on the South Bank were taking his photograph. The London Eye appeared in the background.

'I'm fine. I just don't check my messages every half-hour,' Anita said.

'How much will this cost? Calling your mobile in Bulgaria?' Veronica asked.

'Same as if I was in London,' Anita replied.

'*Were* in London.'

Anita took a deep breath. For God's sake. She went to all this trouble not to be there and people never left her alone. She wished she had been born in the age of trunk calls and red telephone boxes with multiple windowpanes. She imagined Veronica pressing button 'A' with a leather-gloved finger.

The silver one had come out of his pose and was talking to the interviewer. He slouched and stuck his hands inside the doublet. His lips moved, revealing flashes of yellowish teeth and the pink inside of his mouth.

'Anita, are you still there? Just don't leave it until the last minute. It would be absurd if all the flights turned out to be booked up,' Veronica said.

'They won't be. I promise.'

'Have you checked availability? It's pointless to promise. Get on with it.' Veronica drew an exasperated breath. 'The wedding rehearsal is next Thursday. We're meeting for lunch at the Pheasant at one o'clock.'

Getting something in the diary was reality creation for Veronica. Those handwritten times and scrawls made with a sharp pencil were ghosts with flesh that would certainly materialise. Ideally, she should be in charge of everyone's diary. Then the world would run properly. Veronica suspected that Anita harboured thoughts of not

135

turning up. That was why she kept mentioning it. The wedding clock ticked.

'What is a wedding rehearsal, anyway?' Anita asked.

Veronica had already explained dispensations, or blessings, to her daughter. Anita hadn't listened to the ins and outs. Barney was going along with wedding fuss for Kendra's sake and Veronica and Howard were going along with it for Barney's.

'As the words suggest, it's a rehearsal for the wedding.' Veronica paused. 'They have them in America.'

For once, she sounded faintly embarrassed. Gotcha, Anita thought.

'Barney's been married before. He doesn't need one, does he?' Anita asked. 'They should go to the register office. And dispense with that clock.'

'I don't know anything about a clock,' Veronica said.

'On the website. It does my head in.'

'Oh, really, Anita. And do remember it's cold here. Don't turn up in one of your Peaseblossom rig-outs as if it were midsummer. The tent will be heated, but . . .'

The telephone conversation with Veronica came to an end, unresolved.

By Anita's age, Veronica had had three children and was powering through her career. Every stage in life was a time of reckoning. Veronica never ceased to calculate the interim profits. Anita tried to second-guess the figures but came up with nothing substantive. She had had jobs in two vintage clothes shops, a Portobello Road coffee bar, a gallery in Islington that sold contemporary ceramics, a catering company, an employment agency specialising in the arts . . . None of the businesses existed any more. Joe Brabazon-Morley's gallery where she currently worked had been established in 1979 and was still going. That was progress, wasn't it? Her boyfriends, in a list, were . . . No, stop it. She turned the sound back on.

The silver statue was saying, 'I mean bodies are washed up by the Thames on a regular basis.' He waved towards the tourists. 'These people don't know the sad side of London. They're just passing through. I get upset every time. That's me. It's the way I am.'

Kendra fitted into the family. She would be a perfect Mostyn daughter-in-law. As had been Harriet, Barney's first. Veronica had no trouble in absorbing serial wives. Kendra was American. She worked in the same firm of management consultants as Barney but on the softer side, PR or HR – Anita hadn't been listening. Physically, Kendra was not dissimilar to Harriet, short but stately with a bum like a bustle, though Harriet had used hers aerodynamically in a swinging skirt. Kendra was more sedentary. She was young and incredibly fresh, in the way that some American women are, her clothes humming with crispness and the memory of tissue paper. No one would have known she had been taken in adultery. Barney towered over her, smiling sheepishly. He was genial and had a slight paunch these days. Quite possibly he had drugged her.

Anita's worries about the wedding blew in squalls, all from the same direction. She feared the ceremony itself, the being herded in a crowd, gusts of sound and colour; everyone focused on the celebration of coupledom and family. She feared the wait for the bride; the period between the hour having struck and the restless anticipation that could go on, she knew from experience, for up to thirty minutes. Then, even worse, having been upstanding, a further wait, pressed more closely against her suited and hatted neighbours, breathing in their scent and their shaving soap, while the bride did who knows what in the porch. This was the moment when she thought she would faint.

She was haunted by the sound of chiming voices asking her questions; the full peal of prosperous complacency. Her parents' friends, who got their gen from Veronica, had Anita down as a dabbler. In education and the marriage game, she didn't cut it. The men would flirt a bit, though they weren't very good at it; waggling shaggy eyebrows and asking about travel plans. The women would tell her about their children; what a success they were and such fun as well.

Anita saw the guests and the flowers and the twinkling glasses turned to polished fragments – and wondered how it would end. The scene reassembled into a pattern of lights and faces. Chairs were being stacked and tables removed, the coconut matting, scattered with crumbs and rucked in places, exposed for dancing. Anita – aged twenty-five at Barney's first wedding – was standing by a butane gas heater that emitted fumes, her legs bare under a gauzy skirt, the upper part of her body mummified in a black fringed silk shawl. Even her hands were tucked inside.

'Where's Gavin – it is Gavin, isn't it? We're dying to meet him . . . Oh, isn't he here? Where is he then?'

20

Along the front, a string of white lanterns came on. They stretched and dipped in a loopy line until the lights merged into a thread that broke at intervals where bulbs had blown. In the creeping darkness, the Captain Cook began to look like a stage set. New hotels in the town catered for non-residents but their bars were expensive and resembled tarted-up offices. Up the hill were the old men's pubs; the television on, the grandads crammed round a single table. Of the seaside bars, only the Captain Cook remained open for the off season. It had two parts: the permanent building that housed the kitchen and a cavernous bar, and the summer annexe directly opposite, across the beach road. This was an airy, temporary structure on a raised platform, with a tent-like roof and sides that were exposed to the weather. Plastic blinds could be drawn down against wind and rain but for the moment, since it was balmy, they were neatly rolled away. A portable infra-red heater glowed hot and took off the chill. Slim cats, mottled grey tabbies, skulked around the table legs. Every so often, waiters ambled over the road in their wine-coloured waistcoats carrying glasses and dishes, then retreated indoors; costumed figures who mingled and chatted to the barman with their backs towards the customers.

Laurence Beament was sitting at a table by the water-side. The Black Sea swished aimlessly around the rocks below. He had lined up his mobile, a packet of cigarettes and a lighter in front of him. The smoking was a furtive treat, reserved for the gentler pace of the Balkans. He rarely indulged in London.

Equilibrium, never a sure thing, seemed achievable on these slow evenings at the back end of Europe. The anticipation of the bottle of Zagorka beer, then its arrival, later the inevitable plate of *kebapcheta* and chips, the waiting in between each stage. Laurence watched the sea, the swash and backwash of waves, and wondered – or, on one occasion had wondered – whether life was more like the tide going out or coming in. The main drawback to the place was boredom but he knew how to ride it, appreciating evenness because it never lasted.

That particular evening, he was the opposite of bored. He had come to see Mossy. Rattled by Fran, and by Mossy's silence, he had taken a couple of days off work and booked a flight to Varna. He surprised himself with his urgent need to see her. He conjured up Mossy's face, the littleness of it under the bleached punk hair, and the smell of whatever she used; it wasn't scent, more something she washed in – a bit coconut, which he liked. He longed to set eyes on her.

There was something hopeless about Mossy – lost – which made him feel in charge. She beamed charm at him – an odd kind of charm – then, at some point, the light developed a flicker; there was a dip in the grid.

He had hired a car at the airport and driven directly to The Hesperia, without forewarning her. His appearance would be a delightful surprise, he hoped. He imagined her lonely and ready for company. They would laugh at the Captain Cook's menu together. 'Mince pie wit yellow cheese?' he would read aloud. Unfortunately, she had been out.

Laurence was anxious then, expecting she would have returned by dusk. He telephoned but she failed to pick up. The spontaneity of the trip turned faulty. He had to be back at work by the end of the week – and, in the meantime, would have to find a hotel room. He had hoped – Mossy being pliant and desired – that, after a pleasant evening together, he would be able to share his own bed.

Standing in the dimly lit corridor of The Hesperia, he had wondered what to do next, and smoothed the back of his neck repeatedly. Keeping all options open, he sent a text, which said, *How are things? Give a sign. Are you lost?*

Feet approached over the boards. Two people brushed past the end of Laurence's table. The woman had tired eyes and breasts flattened by the pressure of a taut Guernsey sweater. Her companion, a grey-haired man in a waxed jacket, cast a shadow over the seated Laurence as he surveyed the sea. He scanned the view, panning the curved edge where the cliffs met the shoreline with an imaginary camcorder – encountering the blip of the defunct grain silo.

'Yes,' he said, 'with a steady hand I should be able to keep the doofer out of the frame. We'll come back tomorrow in the light.'

Laurence tapped the box of cigarettes, released one and lit it. Having taken a drag, he exhaled slowly and hung his hand over the balustrade, letting the smoke drift away from the eating area. No one at the Captain Cook had ever objected.

After a certain amount of hoo-hah – checking the wind-chill factor, finding their glasses – the couple settled at the next table.

'Where is everyone? I need a drink,' the man announced, hitching his trousers. 'Where's the bloody waiter?' He raised an arm; fingers spread like a sunburst.

143

Laurence reached out for the A4-size vinyl-bound book that was the Captain Cook's menu. He tried matching the words with the tiny bleached photos of dinners but the game was no good on his own. He felt bereft.

'Ah, here comes our chap.' The man in the waxed jacket renewed the sunburst hail.

A waiter was ambling across the beach road. He climbed the platform steps, paused at the top, then sidled over and stood between the two tables, looking out to sea. 'Per-lease,' he said, in a melancholy voice.

The woman in the Guernsey sweater got in quickly. 'Pike-perch and a mixed salad. Keith, have you decided?'

Two cats zigzagged across the floor and began prowling up and down under the table.

'These animals seem to understand English,' Keith said, half turning, including Laurence in the bonhomie. 'That's impressive, isn't it? I think I'd like the pike-perch too.'

Laurence gave a curt nod without making eye contact.

The waiter shook his head, not just to the pike-perch – to existence. He had no pad and wrote nothing down. 'To drink?' His wine-coloured waistcoat was faded, its cloth worn and in need of dry cleaning; one button hung loose.

After supper, Laurence walked along the beach road away from the old part of the town. Here and there, light from apartments interrupted the dusk, though, for the most part, the buildings were in darkness. Once past the last of the locked beach bars, the view opened up and waves rolled in, heavy with coils of seaweed. Sea defences divided the shore from the road; massive L-shaped blocks made of precast concrete. Their arrangement was apparently haphazard – a tower toppled by a giant child – though in reality each slab must have required a winch to be placed into position. The defences looked more threatening than the sea.

The beach road in made-up form ended, marked by a rope strung between two wooden poles. Beyond was a dug-over track and an abandoned digger, tipped at an angle. The Hesperia with its jutting balconies was visible in the distance, set back across shifting dune land. Laurence turned round and walked back to pick up the hired car that he had left in the village square.

Once in the car, he rechecked his phone. There was a message. *All good. Loving your apartment. Might extend stay.* Laurence started the engine and drove fast. Having dallied in the Captain Cook to give Mossy ample time to return, he now sped. He revved up the hill and when he joined the main road, slowed without stopping. He looked over his shoulder to see if anything was coming, then hit the accelerator again.

Billboards by the roadside offering newly built property in Albena rushed past. Fleeting views of white buildings, blue pools, bright price stickers showed up in his headlamps. One or two heavy lorries trundled by in the opposite direction. He took the bumpy access road to The Hesperia at the same speed – and with a screech of brakes, brought the car to a stop in the forecourt. He went up the front steps in two strides.

Laurence hurried through the lobby, along the walkway, down the corridor. He knocked on the door of his apartment. There was no reply.

'It's Laurence, Mossy,' he called.

He dithered. He paced up and down the corridor. After a few minutes, he put his key in the lock and turned it, cautiously. The hallway and the living room were in darkness. He switched on the lights. The blinds were drawn shut, the sofa cushions plumped up. Everything was tidy. Laurence walked across to the windows and raised one of the blinds. He looked out at the garden chairs propped against the table and the low evergreen hedge. The little uplighters around the pool made slender jets of illumination that rose like steam from geysers.

Laurence went into the bedroom, knowing she had gone. He opened drawers and cupboards, banging them. He hated the hollow noise that they made. In the kitchen,

the appliances were off, the fridge door left ajar. The fan whirred pointlessly.

'Where the hell is she?' he said aloud.

He didn't know what to do. Nothing happened but it wasn't the same as *nothing happening*. Instead of the usual reams of lying-down minutes, flat as the dead reading of an EEG monitor, the minutes all stood up to attention and bristled with a life of their own.

21

On the morning of the wedding rehearsal, Anita sent a text to Veronica saying she was back in London. She drank two cups of tea but was unable to eat.

Half an hour before setting out, she amassed a heap of clothes on her bed. She shovelled through the pile, cramming weightless garments in parrot-feather colours into her overnight bag.

Outside, the refuse van stopped and started along the street, its orange lights revolving and flashing. Their reflections bounced around the walls of the flat. The machinery groaned and clattered.

Her phone beeped. Anita assumed it was a message from her mother. Veronica would be fussing about something. She picked up the phone. The message was from Laurence: *Please send photos ASAP. Can't wait any longer. L.*

When the van moved away the room stopped vibrating and the light show ended. A dog barked. Anita looked out of the front window. The day was grey and early-looking. Ivor was trundling his wheelie bin from the other side of the street. Lily leapt behind him, excited by the open lid that clattered.

'That's a takeaway glued to the bottom. Who are these fuckers who use my bin? Last week it was animal remains,' Ivor said to Anita who had joined him on the pavement.

'What kind of animal?' she asked.

'Some furry thing with a tail.' Ivor flipped the lid over with a bang. 'The Albanians process motile rubbish only. They wear those fat gloves but they're purely ornamental. I'll be plying the shovel as usual, arse over tip. Scrape, scrape, scrape.'

'*Are* they Albanian?'

'I presume so. I hear them muttering to each other,' Ivor said.

The refuse van down the road whined into action again. They waited for the din to pass.

'When's the staycation over?' Ivor asked.

'It's not a staycation. I told you, Ivor. I've been taking photographs.'

Ivor paused and brushed his hands on the seat of his trousers. 'I thought you were having a rest.'

'A rest?'

'Yeah, you look like you need one. You haven't got much colour.'

A fine mist of builder's sand skimmed over the pavement and settled like early snow.

'You're an arty type, aren't you?' Ivor continued.

'I wish,' Anita said. 'I was hopeless at art. We had this art teacher at school who was ultra-precious. "Outlines are bogus. You do not have one. Neither do I."' She was jabbering on. Ivor was staring at her. 'Then someone found out that he painted these massive canvases of red and black targets with naked girls in the bullseyes. My friend Fran said we should complain.'

'Nah. Not a sackable offence,' Ivor said. 'Bit of fun in his spare time. You should have chalked targets on the back of his jacket. I can't stand all that PC bollocks. No, I just thought – the photography, the clothes – the hair.'

'Oh, that was a bit of a mistake,' Anita said.

'Reminds me of a girl. Erin Killick. She set about her scalp with a pair of scissors when her sister died. She came into school with tufts all different lengths.'

'Thanks,' Anita said.

Ivor scrutinised her, losing eye contact as he peered at the top of her head. 'It's different to Erin's. Long time ago now. School. Funny the stuff you remember. Clearer than yesterday, the past. Much clearer.' He paused. 'If you ever need anything, just bang on the door.'

Lily was already up the front path, sticking her narrow nose through the letter-box flap.

Anita went back into the house. Sand had found a way into the hall and also into her living room; it mingled with the dust on the floorboards. Two leaves from a plane tree had also drifted in. She picked up her phone and reread Laurence's message.

He had said, at the Chelsea dinner, that the houses she photographed need not be for sale – the aspect of the project that had baffled her father. Their images were to whet the appetite; a mere first stage in a process. To choose property was to dream. It was wish-fulfilment of those night-time dreams of discovering rooms. She could take the logic a step further. That wasn't so terribly wrong, was it?

Anita hit reply. She blamed a technology glitch for her delay and admitted she was hopeless. She schmoozed Laurence a bit, calling him Larry, 'angel', which was probably a mistake, and said how incredibly sweet and forbearing he was. *Sending them now*, she ended.

The train from Waterloo, the slow service, took about an hour and fifteen minutes. It pottered through the countryside and made frequent stops in suburban places. The doors wheezed open and shut as passengers got on and off. Anita knew the names of the stations off by heart. She picked up a discarded copy of *Metro* from the opposite seat and turned over the pages without reading.

At Andover, an elderly driver from Emerald Cabs was waiting for her. Anita got in the back seat on the passenger side and gradually set like cement. The driver talked but she didn't listen. Road restrictions and sets of temporary traffic lights held them up for a while, then the roads cleared. Gates and hedges, fields and gardens passed by, dull and luminous in brown winter light. Anita looked out on a landscape that was indifferent to her but swallowed her up. She was delivered to the Pheasant.

As Anita paid the fare, she heard familiar voices. Car doors were opening and shutting. People she knew stood on the bumpy piece of land opposite the pub. There was Kendra smiling and laughing with Veronica. Barney with his best man, old school friend, Charlie Burroughs. The Chevening cousins with their little girls. Two women whom Anita didn't recognise – maybe friends of Kendra – were talking together. An older woman, immaculately made-up and dressed in a beige suit, emerged from the back seat of a car. She was probably Debs, Kendra's mother. Everyone was greeting each other.

The cab drove away. It disappeared round the bend. Anita was separated from the others by the road. A van went by, pulling a trailer of fir trees. In a minute, someone would see her. Having said she had 'returned', she couldn't go back. This is what makes children scream and wail, 'Please. Please. I didn't *mean* it.' The non-rewinding of the clock. The having moved on to the next thing, which, in an inadvertent moment, she had let happen. She retied the belt of her coat until it compressed her.

In a rush of noise, Barney and Charlie crossed the road, between passing cars. Both whooped when they spotted Anita and, one after another, crushed her in a hug.

'Where's the Peugeot, Netticles?' Barney asked.

'In for repair,' she said.

'Bad luck,' Barney said. 'Probably time you replaced it, isn't it?'

22

The Pheasant wasn't the nearest pub to St Michael and All Angels but it was old and covered in creeper. Stickers on the windows, bleached by sunlight, showed that the food had been recommended in a guide, five years previously. Inside, a series of small rooms interconnected, some up a step, some down. The ceilings were low and the men had to dip their heads as they filed through the shallow openings that joined one part to another.

The wedding party made their way to a room at the back. Tables were rearranged so that they could sit together as a group. A fire in the grate scented the air with wood-smoke, turning daytime into evening. Food was chosen. The men returned to the bar to buy drinks and order. Betsy and Alice, aged seven and four, glowed pink as they waited.

Barney suggested they should have a photo-free afternoon. 'Save all that for the wedding.' His tone of voice was more orotund than it had once been. Put on for the occasion – or a sign of middle age; Anita didn't know which. The affability had always been there. Now Barney's age matched it. She hadn't seen her brother for months.

'I do so agree, darling,' Veronica called back. 'What is memory for?'

And the atmosphere in the absence of guests, hats, cameras, was carefree, two days before the event. The noise levels rose. Bad luck for the other clients who had chosen this day for a peaceful lunch in the Pheasant. Barney smiled at Kendra and she smiled back, as though it were an ordinary afternoon. Betsy and Alice wolfed down adult-sized portions of teriyaki beef skewers.

Talk moved to and fro, passed with the bread basket, and hardly touched Anita. She tucked herself in a corner seat – tapestry cushion on slippery wood – and watched the fire, or the children. No one was surprised that she had made it back from Varna in time. They weren't much interested in Bulgaria.

Then it was time to leave. They gathered belongings, found coats, put them on. Howard went to settle the bill. They carried on talking – louder than ever, now fuelled by booze – as they walked through the rooms, past random people, locals and visitors. Finally, they were outside and crossing the road to the parking lot. Car doors were flung open. There was space for everyone, if they squashed up, and only a short journey. Anita went with the Chevening cousins. The little girls prodded each other and gave sideways looks at Anita from their car seats.

'Sing it,' Betsy said.

'No. You sing it,' Alice whispered.

'What's the song?' Anita asked. 'Perhaps I know it.'

The girls giggled.

Leaves blew in from the porch and scattered over the worn stone when they all trooped in to St Michael and All Angels, Elvham. They were twenty minutes late. The vicar, a punctual woman who wore a cream-coloured Arran jumper over her clerical shirt, hurried them straight to the front of the church to practise the correct line-up for the ceremony. It was colder inside St Michael's than out and the air smelled of dead grass.

The wedding party recessed. They processed. This was the right order for a rehearsal, Kendra said. Betsy and Alice carried bunches of dried sedum – one each – from the Kingsfold garden; substitute posies.

At the back of the church, an elderly man attached photographs to a display board. He scrabbled noisily in a box and dropped drawing pins that pinged as they hit the stone slabs.

Anita sat on a pew, slightly apart from the others, and

156

tried to stop her teeth from chattering. She kept her scarlet fingerless gloves on. There were two aspects to being there. One was unreal, like a film set. The other was real. There was no reconciling them. She felt alone and longed for a sibling to keep her company. She couldn't escape.

When it came to the ceremony, everyone said their lines with actorly intent; not exactly hamming, but with a panache that might be missing on the day. You could see their breath in the air. And they didn't mean it less, in their own clothes, on a Thursday, without a congregation. The words didn't take effect, that was all.

Howard stood in for Ed Scott, Kendra's father. Ed had a meeting in New York to attend and wouldn't be arriving until Saturday. Debs's partner, Yanni, was stuck at the airport in Athens. The Scotts were divorced and lacked a solid centre, which was why the wedding was taking place in Elvham. Howard gave Kendra away as if she were his own daughter. He stood upright beside her in his polished shoes. Anita shivered and looked fondly at her father.

The vicar informed them in advance that she would stop short of the pronouncement and when she came to the point, gave the couple a nice smile. Barney kissed Kendra; the kind of rueful kiss that you would give in front of family. When it was over, they wandered back down the aisle, holding hands. Betsy and Alice stopped being good and raced around, knocking over the little chairs that the Sunday school sat on. The vicar, who had made up ten of her lost twenty minutes, stopped to chat to the elderly man with the drawing pins. The photographs were of a village in Swaziland.

A field on the other side of Gee's Lane had been commandeered for guests' parking. Howard's notices were nailed in place on the gateposts. One by one, the cars bypassed the field and turned into the drive of Kingsfold House, crowding it out.

Indoors, flowers were everywhere. Inky dahlias and crimson chrysanthemums splayed loosely in jugs and vases; pieces of greenery were strewn on the floor, as though work were still in progress. Through the open back door, as more people trooped in, Anita heard the wedding tent on the lawn creak like an iceberg.

23

Returning from the wedding rehearsal at St Michael and All Angels, Veronica laid on kitchen tea. Out came everyday biscuits from the big square tin and a bought Dundee cake. Earl Grey in two teapots; one brown, one ancestral. The room smelled of the previous evening's fish supper. Outside was dark and inside full of voices, as if it were Christmas but without the fuss. Talk was of current affairs and City gossip. Charlie Burroughs, with his squeeze-box face, impersonated the Chancellor of the Exchequer giving the autumn budget. Someone – was it Kendra? – described a new production of *The Winter's Tale*.

'Not my favourite play. All that oracle business,' Veronica said. 'There's supposed to be a silent version, a 1910 film. Apart from "Exit pursued by a bear", how could that possibly work?'

The conversation fitted together like a jigsaw puzzle – supposedly of the outside world but confined to the kitchen table. There was nothing to disturb. Parts of the house had dark corners that were less hospitable. Colonial photos of men in turbans playing polo; heavy curtains that concealed the vacuum cleaner. Anita felt unsafe in the room with the stove and the crowded dresser; lamps lit under red shades.

Even before Barney's phone rang, Anita was afraid. She had a sense – quite distinct – that to step out of the pool of light was dangerous. It wasn't a premonition, but she knew, in a reversion to childish thinking, that safety has a circumference.

Barney left the table and walked to the other end of the room, his head inclined to the phone with business-like attention. His face, angled down, looked full up and jowly. In the doorway to the hall, he turned into a silhouette. Charlie and Howard carried on talking but the pattern was broken. The kitchen clock struck six. Chairs were pushed back and scraped on the floor. Phones were taken out and messages checked; car keys found. Anita continued to pick at crumbly bits of cake.

The call was from a wedding guest, Milla Chalmers. Milla had been asked to sing Dido, in Purcell's *Dido and Aeneas*, on Saturday evening, replacing a soprano with a throat infection. She would be able to make the wedding but not the reception.

'Well, that ruins the seating plan,' Veronica said, reaching for the book and opening it on scribbled drawings of circles with names spiking out from them; a cosmos of suns.

'Take away a chair.' Howard poured the last drips of conker-coloured tea into his mug and added a slug of milk.

'No, Howard. That never works.' Veronica put on the amber-framed spectacles. 'Barney, darling. Jeremy Fernyhough: have we put him next to Renate for a particular reason?'

Barney sat down again.

Occasions have a natural length and this was an add-on. A coda to a piece that didn't need one. The Chevening cousins, Charlie, Debs and Kendra's friends were ready to leave. Shoes tapped on the stone-flagged floor. Belongings were assembled.

The ones who were going insisted that nobody move. They didn't want to break up the party. They would see everyone again on Saturday.

'Gosh, the wedding!' Barney said, as if he had forgotten that was why they were there.

Anita should have gone too – into the drawing room or up to her bedroom – but she stayed at the table. The festive atmosphere – after the front door finally banged shut and the cars turned out of the drive on to Gee's Lane – was replaced by something more weary and functional.

Anita missed Betsy and Alice. She glanced at the place where they had been sitting. Children were more alive than adults. No reality check was necessary for them – they swam in the substance, though madly. Betsy and Alice had inhabited those chairs, wriggling and pushing with their feet against the table legs; no mere sitting. Their plates were tiny worlds. Ingredients of the fruit cake they hadn't liked – bits of candied peel and burnt currants, spat out initially and afterwards dissected – were arranged in formation: family groups, dances, circuses, shoppers and shopkeepers. Anita hadn't entirely lost the key. She could see what they were at and had made a few suggestions.

The talk at the end of the table was becoming more animated. 'If we put so and so here, then . . .' Veronica jabbed at the master plan.

They suddenly loved the challenge. Sudoku mixed with character analysis.

'But they're both dull. We can't put two dull—'

'I've never found Sorrel dull. She knows everything there is to know about the Dark Ages – as a discredited construct, that is.'

'Yes, but Noel wouldn't be interested, would he?'

'He went through his own *saeculum obscurum* a few years ago.'

'Really?'

'When was the *saeculum obscurum*, anyway? I've never known.'

'Petrarch started it. He said they'd just emerged.'

'No, that's not right. It was Caesar Baronius. He was referring, among other things, to the sexual activity of the popes.'

'Are you sure about that? That can't be right. Who was Caesar Baronius? Why have I never heard of him?'

'He was an Italian cardinal who wrote church history.'

'He's already got Keziah on his right.'

'She's not a bundle of laughs.'

Anita had always been on the sidelines of family discussions. She had learned to think like the Mostyns – but without the brain power. What was the good of intellectualising, as a method of thinking, if you didn't have the backup?

She had hoped, in loving Gavin Peace, that she was on to something different; a new take on life. She had, in the end, struggled to follow him too. And later struggled against the evidence that Gav also, though Zen, liked the sound of his own voice.

Anita glanced across the table. Her brother Mark was there; standing behind the girls' vacant chairs. She found herself holding a fragment of cake, squashing it like a fly between middle finger and thumb. The others were occupied, talking and rearranging names on the paper. She blinked. The red shades were too red. They cast the wrong glow.

163

He was leaning forward – in some way precarious – poised between uprightness and instability. Compared to Barney, he was young; trapped in the age she had last seen him. At first, she couldn't make out what he was holding, but, as she watched, he changed his grip and something made of glass caught the light. One hand lifted and passed over the other. Encountering nothing but air, it moved to and fro, hovering in a strange benediction. The mistiming, though small, shocked her; the blatant incompetence of it.

He attempted the movement again and the second time aimed right. His hand clamped over the top of a small bottle. He began to unscrew it. The operation was slow and ragged. It pained her to watch. His fumbling ended with a jerky movement that almost upturned the bottle. Colourless liquid splashed on to the table. A few drops went into the china mug decorated with green flowers that Alice had been drinking from. Anita's stomach pitched. It was as though she had surfaced in the night and come up to that level where unconsciousness and consciousness swill around together and dreams are partly controlled. A vile thread connected her with Mark's actions. Everything she had ever been happy about vanished.

Mark put the bottle to his lips. Having drained it, he picked up the mug with a clumsy left hand. He drank from that too. Alice wouldn't have wanted this drunk uncle to put his mouth where hers had been.

The others continued to talk at the far end of the table; their voices like echoes in a tunnel.

A howl of laughter brought Anita back to herself.

'Mother, that is preposterous,' Barney was saying. 'I won't let you get away with that.'

Family discussion was all based on chiming in. What did chiming in require? Anita could shove up and take an interest in the seating plan. Surely, among all Veronica's scribbles, she would recognise some names. But she lacked credibility. The others left her alone at the end of the table. Who was Renate, anyway? Anita moved her plate to one side, folded her arms where the plate had been and rested her head. No one noticed. Ivor said she needed a rest. She was having one. Voices droned on.

Behind her closed eyelids, a mote of light, sharper and brighter than any floater, appeared, like a glint in glass, and held steady. There was no safety anywhere. Anita saw herself leaving her bedroom and walking across the top landing. She heard the click as she switched on the bathroom light, and the swoosh from the cold tap.

She rinsed her face and swallowed some water. She switched the light off.

Mark was standing with his back to the stairs. Barney's door was shut; Mark's partly open – everywhere dark. The house was asleep.

Anita opened one eye and saw movement in the shadow. Beyond the plates and the mugs, someone stirred. The rocking had begun. To and fro movements so slight she disbelieved them; then the sigh – a calm giving up – like a baby's in prelude to sleep. Slowly, she raised her head from the table. Sleep was best – but not yet. The stairs were behind him. Anita willed her brother to take a step forward. She put all her effort into it – as if effort made a difference.

Mark looked at her. He made an attempt at speaking, his mouth opened and shut again. Then he got it out. 'Can you drive me home, Anita? Please.'

'No,' Anita shouted, as her brother tipped over.

The talking trickled to a stop.

A series of tumbling thuds set the house throbbing. Wood splintered as the banisters at the turn of the stairs cracked open. Then the dive through air as he fell.

She began to cry. At first, dry sobbing, then tears came.

Chairs scraped and china smashed on the floor. An overhead light was switched on. Hands covered her.

'It was all that last-minute travelling,' someone said. 'She only got back from Bulgaria this morning. I told her to leave herself plenty of time.'

24

Ed Scott, Kendra's father, and Yanni, Debs's new partner, had never met but, American and Greek, among the Mostyns and Randalls, they joked about the rain and cuffed each other on the back. Good luck to him, Ed thought. He was glad Debs had someone to take care of her.

Granny Randall, aged ninety-eight, looked splendid in a red velvet hat with black trim. Under a man's umbrella and holding a strange arm, she experienced stretches of vacancy – chasms that opened up. Everyone said how marvellously she was doing and that tided her over; little bridges from lucid to lucid. After the service, the photographer rounded people up as though herding cattle through a gate. He eased them into place with a slow shove. The light was poor but, against the yew trees and the grey stone of the church, the multicoloured umbrellas looked cheerful.

The guests drank steadily all afternoon and into the evening. By eight o'clock it was all a bit of a shambles; the younger element – teenage cousins – cruised round the marquee, knocking over any stackable ballroom chair that wasn't occupied. The tinies pulled on the ropes and covered themselves in cake. Everyone was caught in eddies of noisy conversation. Somehow, Veronica had got hold of a dilapidated marquee held up in the old-fashioned way. People said what a lovely old tent – and decried newer models with Gothicised plastic windows – but none of them had been brought up on poles and ropes, except for the elderly who mostly left after tea, and several guests tripped over, or banged themselves, and had to drink more to recover. Outside, it carried on raining, hammering on the tent roof.

Howard made some attempt at dividing day from night by calling instructions about the dinner seating plan. His voice came across as a distant rumble, half on the mic, half off. Catering staff filed in with trays of cutlery and glasses and, like disciplined scene-shifters in a chaotic production, got on with laying the tables.

The starter was greeted with enthusiastic whoops and a slow handclap – or so it seemed to Ed Scott. Late arrivals, friends of the bride and groom, holding coats over their heads, having run from their cars, made apologetic grimaces while they shook off the rain. Ed, who had failed to notice their entrance, was perplexed – but the whole day had been perplexing. Part of the roof was leaking. Someone had brought a pail. Where had Veronica found this relic of a tent? It was rigged like a tea clipper. He took a second look at his portion of salmon mousse to see if that explained the applause. Did it conceal a firework? He did business with the British and knew their fondness for simple pranks. No one on the top table had clapped. Veronica, on Ed's deaf side, was engaged in conversation with Charlie, Barney's best man. Kendra, on his good side, leant forward to talk with Debs down the row.

For a moment, Ed had time to himself. He looked up and saw a woman – the last of the latecomers – standing in the open flap of the tent; darkness and lashing rain behind her. She stared without looking, as if the scene in front of her had no meaning – was an optical illusion that would never assemble into a pattern of lights and faces.

Ed half rose in his seat. Veronica sensed the movement and glanced at him. Maybe she feared he was about to make a speech. He smiled, shook his head and settled back. Veronica resumed her conversation with Charlie.

Ed wondered whether the woman at the entrance was Barney's sister, Anita. She woke up unwell, they said. She may show up later. Her absence wasn't made much of. This lot were breezy – and good at prioritising. A little sickness wouldn't stand in their way. But they didn't want further questions; that much was evident. They made it clear he wasn't family. Though they weren't unfriendly, they shut him out with that mixture of eloquence and aloofness he recognised as English. He could talk with the best of them; had quite a reputation in that direction. But the verbal sonatina the Mostyns and their kind hid behind, he just didn't get it. Fluent and confident, they played for hour upon hour. OK, so we know you know that one; let's start on the music.

Kendra got on with Barney's parents pretty well – and liked them. She hadn't seen much of Anita. Netticles, Barney called her. Someone else mentioned Mossy. Ed figured out it was the same person. Unless there was also a Mossy and a Netticles upstairs in bed! There had been a brother who had died following an accident. A car accident, Ed guessed. It had happened some years back – but what a tragedy for the family. He had nothing but sympathy for them – and felt ashamed of his censure, though it had been good-humoured.

He had been looking forward to meeting Anita. She kept herself apart. She was a bit of a rebel maybe. He had that impression. He would have liked to tell the story of his own rebellious horse. Kendra had heard it. Maybe he would tell Veronica if he got an opportunity.

He had been around ten years old at the time and had

stopped to read the day's pages in the open Bible in the glass box outside the Baptist chapel in his home town. *For they are a rebellious horse*, he read in the Book of the Prophet Ezekiel – this was followed by stirring stuff about the noise of wings and the noise of wheels and a noise of a great rushing. He identified with whoever heard those noises because he sometimes had rushing in his head when his parents criticised – but most of all he identified with the horse. He had a rebellious horse inside him. He came from a Bible-reading family but no one had mentioned the horse or told him how to look after it. They said he should learn to behave himself. For the whole day he lived with the concept of the horse and in the evening he went back to the Baptist chapel to have another look. It was dark by then – a winter evening – and the glass box wasn't lit up. He had to wait for someone to go in or out of the shop next door to see the print clearly.

For they are a rebellious . . . he read. The street lamp was humming – the tube about to go, not yet gone. Light streamed from the open door as a man walked out with his purchases. *House*, Ed read, peering, and felt sick with disappointment. *House.*

Not everyone he told got that story.

Ed watched the woman who stood at the tent flap – the guests and the flowers and the twinkling glasses like polished fragments – and thought she looked pale. Then she focused. She smiled at someone she recognised and made her way to their table.

He saw her later in the evening when dinner was over. Chairs were being stacked and tables removed. The coconut matting was exposed for dancing; scattered with crumbs and rucked in places. She was standing by a butane gas heater that was emitting fumes, her legs bare under a gauzy skirt and the upper part of her body wrapped in a green silk shawl.

He went over and introduced himself. 'Hi. I'm Ed Scott, Kendra's father.'

The band clattered about the dais, firing off salvos of bass chords, blundering into the mic. He didn't quite catch her reply. It wasn't maybe the best thing to say but he said it anyway. 'How're you doing?'

'Brilliant.'

'Good.' Ed nodded and glanced down at her fascinating skirt. When he raised his eyes, she was looking in a different direction.

'Kendra is beautiful, isn't she?' she said.

'Yes, indeed,' he said.

Anita was also beautiful. Overly thin perhaps, with bones that seemed glass brittle. He wanted to treat her gently – and guessed he would feel the same even without knowing she had just got up from her sickbed.

'These days of celebration have a momentum. It's not so easy to join in at the end. The blessing service was great. One of Kendra's friends – I didn't catch her name – sang a Handel aria. She had a lovely soprano voice. Maybe someone made a recording. You'll be able to check it out.' Ed leant forward and patted Anita on the shoulder. 'I'm glad you showed up. I've been looking forward to meeting you.'

She seemed a little taken aback by the gesture – though not panic-stricken. He forgot, sometimes, that he was elderly and not as attractive as he used to be.

'Actually, I was only invited for the evening do,' she said. 'And then we were late. It was really embarrassing. I came with Will and Anastasia. Will's always late. He sets out at the time he should be arriving and then pretends he's in shock.'

Ed leant forward to catch what she said. 'So you're not family?'

'No.' She laughed.

'You're standing dangerously close to that heater.' Ed looked down at the pieces of flimsy cloth that overlapped like the petals of an inverted flower. Earlier he had wanted to kneel down and touch them. Now he was less sure. 'Don't move suddenly, will you?'

He smiled and moved away.

Ed needed the bathroom. He made his way across the floor, taking care because of the unevenness. He thought of the grass underneath the matting; the November programme of leaf sweeping and treating worm casts. Maybe, on a fine, frost-free day, they would mow one last time with the blades set high. He had once been a mower of lawns. When he and Debs and Kendra, their only child, lived in New Jersey they had had a good one. These days he lived in an apartment.

Outside, it was still raining, but diminished to a fine drizzle. He wouldn't get a soaking. A path of duckboards had been laid to the back door, the edges uncertain in the night. It was a fine old house; the plain windows regularly spaced, two pairs flanking the door and three rows of five above. There was an identical arrangement at the front, though 'front' had no meaning in a house so relentlessly two-faced. Another odd feature was the absence of steps. The doors were flush with the ground. This gave the building an appearance of top-heaviness, as if the bottom few feet had been forced below the surface by a giant hand that pressed on the roof.

No security lighting came on as Ed approached. He needed to watch his footing. Rain pattered on his head and on the stiff cloth of his morning coat. A lamp had been left on in the hall. Through a kitchen window he saw the catering staff still toiling away. The upper floors were dark. Ed had no idea of the internal layout, though the pleasing clean lines of the house suggested a single central staircase and a simple arrangement of rooms on each floor. Barney's sister was up there somewhere. Having mistaken her identity, she seemed to him doubly missing.

Part Two

1

At the time of Barney's first wedding, Anita was independent of the Mostyns and living with Gavin.

'I've been wanting a piece of stiff card for a while,' Gav had said when the invitation arrived. 'Nice of Mr and Mrs Roger Cook from Berkshire to send one. Who the fuck are they?'

Anita thought that he might concede to go to the reception but not to the church. Gav wasn't against God – those books by Krishnamurti and Jung – but he would never sit in a pew. For a party, the white suit would come out. He would have been conspicuous, therefore, and might have chosen to turn on the charm. He could dance – which was more than could be said for her brothers, who had unlearned rhythm at prep school.

In the event, Gavin had gone to Tangier, which didn't count as outright refusal. Anita had never found out how to make another person do or not do something. She was too tolerant, Fran said. 'Don't let him go off on his own, Mossy. Assert yourself.' But Anita hated insistence and part of her was relieved that, for the family occasion, she wouldn't have to splice herself between Gav and the Home Counties.

She had not been to Elvham for months. The hawthorn was out in the hedgerows. London had settled into summer but in Hampshire the white and green haze of spring hung about the fields. As she drove along Gee's Lane and through the open gates of number fifteen, she tried to remain detached. Sturdy and elegant, Kingsfold House predated the Mostyns and would see them off. It had never taken sides in her difficulties.

She heard the piano as soon as she got out of her car. It was belting out chords and glissandi, as if its insides had turned outwards and the hammers were clapping on the mahogany casing. As she walked round the side of the house, she recognised the opening bars of 'Land of Hope and Glory', not because she had drawn closer, though she had, but because the furious random banging had actually resolved – if such a word were applicable – into that leaden tune. The pianist had reached 'Wider still, and wider' as she went in through the back door.

A copper jug of dark purple lilac stood on the hall table, the stems crammed together and the blooms toppling from them, like a miraculous aberration. Anita put down her overnight bag at the foot of the stairs. The door of her father's study was ajar. Through the gap she could see a neat pile of books standing on the desk, the top one stamped with the ex libris label of the London Library.

Mark – it had to be Mark on the piano – wouldn't hear her footsteps on the hall floor, nor would anyone else in that din. A straightforward set of greetings was what she longed for; some sense of normality. She knew she held such a hope whenever a welcome failed to materialise. Often there was some kind of mild commotion. 'Oh, Anita, I'm just in the middle of . . .' or visitors she hadn't been warned about, talking in the drawing room. She never learned, or armed herself, though her defences were solidly constructed. She had, in the back of her mind, a kind of dolls' house family that remained in place, the mother waiting for her arrival.

There wasn't even a dog, Viking having died of old age the previous winter. Veronica had postponed acquiring and training a new puppy until the wedding was over. Anita was shocked by Viking's absence. She expected him. He had brought out the best in the Mostyns. Being a good dog was enough. He didn't have to excel.

The piano lived in the coatroom, a high-ceilinged cuboid with a single long window; its dimensions were generous for coats but small for a piano. When the upright – a

Challen – arrived, after the death of one of Veronica's aunts, space was found for it there, opposite the row of hooks. The Mostyn collection of elongated, framed photographs of school-boys and military men was raised higher, well above eye level, so that boots or the cross-legged in the front row were all that a glance took in.

The room had a particular smell; the inside of trains mixed with musty humanity. Mark, with one bare foot pumping the pedal, sat on the stool that long ago had swivelled to its lowest point and stuck. His hair was cut shorter than Anita had ever seen it; an old-style barber's cut, shaved up the neck, that revealed the white skin of his scalp. The curls had gone.

'Netticles? Is that you?' He carried on playing, eyelids lowered.

Anita stood to one side of the Barbours and mackintoshes and waited. Sheepskins, windproof jackets, wool coats and Harris tweed coats jostled together; navy blue, olive green, camel and black. They had continued to accumulate after the Mostyn children left home. The ones on wooden hangers looked smug. Most were suspended by hook from the upper thoracic region with their shoulders collapsed in defeated postures. Veronica didn't hold with dry-cleaning for outerwear. She said it took the stuffing out and recommended the whack of a clothes brush.

Mark's hands moved over the keys into new territory, senseless at first; a kind of bar-room vamping that left 'Land of Hope and Glory' trailing. A whiff of scent and cigarette smoke from a lusher tradition was struck out of them. Mark dropped the volume to a whisper and eased off the pedal. He played through the verse of 'Bewitched' – an old favourite of his – and when he reached the chorus began first to hum and then sing.

He stopped abruptly, his fingers spread over the keys. 'I can't *play*. I can't bloody *play* any more.'

'Sounded fine,' Anita said. 'They weren't the right words, though, were they?'

He crashed his hands down in a discord. 'I can't actually *play* any more.'

Jesus, she thought.

He still hadn't looked at her. She might have been one of the coats. His suggestion that she should call in on him in Hammersmith had not resulted in an invitation. She hadn't expected one.

Mark stood up and placed an elbow on the top of the piano in what she recognised as an old attitude. His profile was as well defined as a woodcut. Little folds had formed below the deep eye sockets. He looked more donor than Madonna now he was older – worldly and glum. He was in his thirty-first year and worked for a bank.

'You are spot on, Netticles. The music was Rodgers' but the lyrics weren't Hart's. I'm no longer wild or beguiled so I changed them.' He paused. 'Peace not here?'

'No,' Anita said.

'No? Mother *did* mention something. The Peace that passeth all understanding. Where's he gone? Do you know?'

'Mark, you're being incredibly obnoxious.'

'Oh, sorry, sorry, Netta. We're allies aren't we? You're my only ally. If you love him, I'm sorry.' He put on a fake sad face, swelling out the lower half, making it round as a tulip bulb. 'You're examining me. What do you see?' he asked.

'I'd recognise you anywhere,' she said.

'I'm not my best. Tired and old.' He stretched out his hand and clasped hers. 'Have you come to rescue me from this dire occasion?'

'It will be dire, won't it?' she said.

'A real wedding of a wedding. Why's he doing it? Barney never used to be dull, did he? Or am I misremembering?'

'You were both incredibly dull.'

He smiled.

'When did you get here?' Anita asked.

'Hours ago. Mother's fussing. I took refuge in the walk-in wardrobe.' He relinquished her hand. 'Do you remember when the Bollards came over and we captured their twin boys? I made them eat whatever they found in the coat pockets. I was Fagin. "So, you wanted to get away, my dear, did you?" One of them squealed like a stuck pig and tried to bite me. The other seemed not to mind. Coins, fluff balls, used tissues, train tickets – they all went down the hatch. I wore Mr Bollard's astrakhan hat as a beard. Don't you remember?'

'No.'

'Barney was Barney, as he had a cold and could do the voice. I was Fagin. "Bolter's throat as deep as you can cut. Saw his head off." I suppose you were Nancy.'

'Or the dog?'

'No, Viking was the dog,' Mark said.

The back door banged. Anita heard the sound of voices from the direction of the kitchen.

'Plausible,' she said. 'I'm going to look for someone else to say hello to.'

2

'We're going out to eat,' Veronica said. 'We're so rarely all together.'

Anita hadn't reckoned with a family outing the evening before Barney's wedding, nor with sitting in the back seat of the Volvo between her two brothers. They could have walked the half-mile into Elvham but rarely did, as Gee's Lane was without a pavement. Harriet, Barney's first bride, wasn't with them, of course. She was pretending to be virginal in her parents' house in Berkshire.

When they were all squashed in tight, Barney, with his arm across the back seat, ruffled Anita's shoulder-length hair. He commented on the colour – chocolate at the time. It had covered so much of the spectrum. He and Mark talked over the top of her; the usual blend of jokes and joshing. Jammed between them, Anita had an unnerving sense of them as men; the smell and the size of them. Their legs took up all the space. Mark's right knee and Barney's left pointed towards each other, nearly touching, hemming her in. She felt as if trapped between off-duty military personnel. But they were her brothers. She renewed the notion – and updated it.

Those journeys down through France to La Marjolaine, summer after summer. Anita had hated them. She went into a trance around Winchester and came out of it when the car joined the first French motorway. Since the boys wanted to be next to each other, she travelled on the wing, in the path of speeding Citroëns. Veronica, also on the passenger side of their right-hand-drive car, was impervious to danger and, in any case, second in line for the rear-end hit. Howard devised quizzes based on ancient and modern history and, although the source of knowledge was inside his head, after the first half-dozen questions would cast around for inspiration.

'Da-ad. Please watch where you're going.' Anita had flinched every time and ended on the lap of the brother who was next to her.

'Get off, Anita!'

What had her father hoped to see, as he looked about? A passing cathedral spire, a place name that triggered a memory? No one else bothered that he drifted. All three of them – Veronica, Mark and Barney – were intent on being the first to say, 'The Edict of Fontainebleau.'

As Howard parked, backing the Volvo into a space

by the Elvham War Memorial, Mark took Anita's hand and squeezed it.

Cody's was new to Anita. It had been open for three years, apparently. She remembered it as the butcher's. The Victorian wall tiles had been retained. Panels of trellis softened the starkness. The bullock stared out through green slats.

A young man showed them to their table. Once they were settled, Adam Cody came over to talk, suave in a linen suit, a silk handkerchief tucked into his pocket. He knew all about the wedding and asked Anita if she were one of the bridesmaids.

'Pigeon grey, the dresses, didn't you say, Mrs Mostyn?'

Veronica congratulated him on his recall while retaining the air of someone who had passed on the information under duress.

'I have a good memory for colour,' Adam Cody said. 'I can carry a shade.'

'Was rat second choice?' Mark said, shifting on the bentwood chair that seemed too small for him. 'I'm relieved rat wasn't chosen. Remind me, who exactly is getting married? Is it Peace and Netticles?'

Adam Cody handed round menus. 'It's interesting isn't it, the way colours change name? "Dove", I suppose, was once popular. My granny always said "fawn" and now it's "cappuccino".' He continued seamlessly into the evening's specials and, at the end, gave them an encouraging smile.

The other diners chatted quietly. Tables occupied the whole of the old shop and extended into the butchering part that had once been hidden behind a wall. Anita, with her back to the front window, guessed the clients were locals. Wearing polo shirts or fun necklaces with matching earrings, they might have been there for morning coffee – that was the age group – though the smell of alcohol, garlic and fish disproved this.

The evening progressed. The starter, the main course. Two bottles of wine. Three. Conversation continued, unbroken. Gavin wasn't mentioned again, nor a multitude of other topics that would cause friction. Barney was relaxed. He talked about work, politics, cricket and golf, his own and the previous year's British Open. Harriet was mentioned, fleetingly. Howard played the host, fussing somewhat. This was his treat. Veronica basked in the company of her sons. When Barney spoke, Mark leant back with the air of someone who listened indulgently but without interest. There was a wary distance between the brothers.

Mark got started on the past. He reconstructed episodes from years back; complicated sequences of events connected with Kingsfold and school. They revolved around Mark. Further Adventures of. The Return of. The Boy Strikes Again. He gathered pace. His gestures became extravagant, his voice, assuming various roles, took on different accents. Old prep school masters, his disastrous penfriend from Dortmund, dons at High Table. Mark rose up and down on the bentwood chair, his hands splayed on the table for support.

Anita had trouble recognising what he was talking about. Some of it was meaningless; she couldn't have been there. Once or twice, something accorded with her own memory, but hers was a different view, as if from a seat with obstructed sight lines. A family's shared past was shaped, in the end, by whoever talked loudest and longest.

Veronica, flirtatious with the boys, threw back her head and laughed. Bizzy was hauled in. Bizzy, for God's sake. The victim of long ago still offered to the lions and mauled. Howard, who had begun to look slightly irritated by the nostalgia wallow, perked up.

'He's probably the finance director of a medium-sized company by now, or on the back benches,' he said.

'Don't be ridiculous, Dad.' The sons fell about, laughing. For the first time that evening, Mark and Barney were in accord. They looked similar to each other; as closely interchangeable as when they were boys.

'Well, he might be,' Howard said. 'The most reviled boy in my year is a bishop.'

They laughed even more.

Anita tasted the old familiarity, with its particular flavour, a unique blend, like a tea. Mark had squeezed her hand. She felt the imprint and put faith in it, even though he appeared to have forgotten about her.

Disconcerted as she was by being among Mostyns again, Anita distanced herself. She looked for the bullock's face in the trellis, or observed Adam Cody chatting his way round the clients. She let the surroundings of Cody's restaurant fall into patterns. She half listened to other people's conversations. She told herself that although she had no one to go back to after the wedding, she had *somewhere* – a place and a life of her own. Gavin would, at some stage, return from Tangier. This saved her from desperation.

Being second best to her brothers had, perhaps, become less relevant now they were all grown-up; just one of those things, like not having thick, dark hair, that there was nothing to be done about. The age difference was a smooth curve; no longer a precipice. Maybe there was a manner of being together as adults. Maybe the blend would alter naturally as the family expanded to include in-laws and children. It was too late for what pension providers call unbroken service, but something could be salvaged. The homecoming, so far, had been doable. Veronica sparkled with goodwill. She hadn't picked on her daughter yet, or drawn attention to her defects.

The dessert menu appeared. Mark waved it away and asked for whisky. The conversation turned to the wedding.

'Harry Dawes was my best man. A good choice,' Howard said. 'He wouldn't be a godfather to any of you, which was a pity. A confirmed atheist. Couldn't bring himself to say the words, even with his fingers crossed.'

'The words *are* very peculiar,' Veronica said.

'The best man's speech is the antithesis of the funeral eulogy,' Mark said. 'It would be amusing to swap them. Raise all the good points at the wedding and trash the man with wild innuendo at the funeral.'

'Usually, a fair gap intervenes between the two occasions. Usually,' Howard said. 'People – those still alive – might not perceive the swap.'

'No such thing as a long-term joke, then?' Barney said.

'*Sub specie aeternitatis*, perhaps. Not our prerogative,' Howard said.

'But don't ask you whose?' Barney said.

'Quite,' replied Howard.

Barney studied the menu. 'What do we think a Paris-Brest Coffee Ring is?' he asked.

'It would be good fun to think of a long-term joke. Set it up, say tomorrow, as it's a memorable day, and then, "Wheee".' Mark drew an arc in the air that headed towards Veronica's water glass.

'Mark, really.' Veronica removed the glass quickly. 'A Paris-Brest is a circle of choux pastry, split in half and filled with confectioner's custard. Coffee flavouring can be vile but I expect Adam's chef uses real coffee. Ask.'

Mark didn't wait for her to finish. 'You'd get the punchline in fifty years' time. Sorry, Mother. But what will Charlie Burroughs say in his speech? Where are the stories to make us smirk as we toy with the cake? What is there to say about Barney? A good all-rounder, a good sportsman, successful, intelligent, decent. No imperfections, as far as one can see . . .' Mark's voice was rising. 'Will he mention brotherly love, do you think?'

Other clients were starting to look round. Adam Cody, slipping a credit card into the hand-held machine, raised an eyebrow.

'Wasn't it something to do with a bicycle race?' Howard said.

'Why did you choose Charlie Burroughs as your best man?' Mark presented an expressionless face to his brother.

'One of my oldest friends,' Barney replied.

'Cool.' Mark's mouth set in a rigid line, as if humming – though he wasn't.

193

'Mm. Might try the Paris-Brest,' Howard said into the silence.

For the rest of the meal, the talk had a prosaic quality; not stilted, or full of pauses, but without energy and therefore different. No one commented on the change that had come over Mark. The effect was abrupt, like a clock failing mid-chime. He was preoccupied in a way that shut everyone else out. And wherever it was he vanished to, you wouldn't want to go there.

Anita's response was boredom with an edge of fury – she couldn't speak for the others. As Mark's sister, she had had years of practice. Times that started out buoyant ended up underwater. She felt as if she were on the seabed in the dark – and tried to pretend it was OK down there with the odd-looking fish. At some point, she would regain enough oxygen to return to the surface.

3

The street lamps were on in Elvham when they left Cody's restaurant. Anita hadn't noticed the day's disappearance. Although it was only half past ten, morning seemed imminent – and with it, Barney and Harriet's wedding. Veronica hurried them to the car. They travelled out of the village and along Gee's Lane, Anita again squashed between her brothers. Barney, Veronica and Howard kept up a low-key conversation. Mark said nothing.

Had she spoken enough? Anita wondered. Had she come across as pathetic, locked up in herself? Her post-mortem habit took over. Then she remembered that the evening had skipped along. She hadn't affected anyone. Whereas . . .

Mark's abrupt melancholy had come too late in the evening to fight off. His mood had fallen on them and they had to find an exit. The car came to a stop on the gravel. They all piled out.

Anita listened for Mark's footsteps behind her as she walked round the side of the house. The others were ahead – had already turned the corner. She heard Veronica shift the watering can to find the back-door key. It scraped on the paving. Mark was dragging his feet. At one point, he tripped, swore at the lack of lighting, and continued.

Indoors, the house smelled of lilac. Shut in for a few hours, the scent had had time to develop. Veronica tweaked a stem that was top-heavy and tried to anchor it against its neighbour. She declared she was off to bed. 'If I hang around down here, I'll think of something that needs to be done. And actually there is nothing to do. I'd just be faffing around.' She turned to Barney. 'You need a good night's sleep, darling.'

'Mark's still outside,' Anita said.

Did Veronica show a flicker of annoyance? If it happened, it was fleeting. She moved to the open back door. Upright against the darkness, an elegant presence, she didn't speak straight away. Her hair, which never needed much attention, had been styled into greater sophistication earlier in the day.

She took a step out. 'We're off to bed, Mark,' she called.

No reply came. She waited, then, with a brief shrug of the shoulders, turned. 'He'll come in.'

This made him sound like the dog. Veronica perhaps missed the late evening ritual of letting Viking into the garden; his disappearance and faithful return.

'I'm not going up yet. I'll wait for Mark,' Anita said.

'Well, you need your eight hours too, Anita.' Veronica

came towards her. She hesitated, then said, 'Don't let Mark drink any more.'

The words were uttered quickly and in a matter-of-fact manner. Her face expressed nothing, leaving her daughter wondering whether she had spoken.

Veronica put a hand on Anita's arm, leant forward and kissed her cheek. 'Good night, darling.'

Anita smiled and hugged her mother.

The garden was dark. A single streak of a cloud stretched low in the sky. One or two stars had appeared. Anita sat on the bench by the back door and kicked off her shoes. Beneath her feet, the stone slabs were warm though the air had cooled. On Gee's Lane, a truck with loose rear doors rattled past the house. A motorbike buzzing to overtake zizzed behind like a wasp trapped in a beer glass. The road snaked in long curves, dangerous for overtaking. Anita listened until the biker took a flying risk on one of the bends and roared away. That left the broken percussion of rattling doors continuing towards Elvham.

Something moved within the shadows. She saw the flash of a white shirt. Her brother emerged, walking towards her across the lawn. She shifted slightly.

'Where have you been?' she asked when he stood in front of the bench.

He said nothing.

'Mark?'

'In the summer house. I sat in an armchair with no springs.' His voice was flat.

'I haven't been in there for years,' she said.

'Full of relics.'

'There was always a lot of stuff in there. I never got past the deckchairs.'

He pulled a hip flask out of his jacket pocket. 'At this moment, some tent monstrosity is sitting in a garden in Berkshire.' He raised the flask to his lips and upended it. 'Empty. Are you looking forward to tomorrow?' he asked in the same dull voice.

'To the wedding? Parts of it will be all right. I never like answering all those questions people ask.'

'Ask them some. "What have you done with *your* life?"' He stood up again. 'I'm going in for a refill. You won't vanish, will you?'

'No. I'll be here. You could get me a glass of something.'

'Good girl.'

He was gone about ten minutes. When he returned the flask was back in his pocket. He was carrying two tumblers and handed her one, then flopped down on the bench beside her.

'Do you remember Brigitte?' Anita asked.

'Not really,' Mark said. 'She was one of the au pairs, wasn't she? Sly eyes. They all had sly eyes.'

'She was bored. Homesick too, maybe. She wrote long letters and kept a journal. Like someone in the nineteenth century. It wouldn't be like that now.'

'What did she say about us?'

'The journal had a lock. It was lavender-coloured plastic and covered in Disney stickers. I tried a penknife on it. No luck. In any case, she wrote in German.'

Mark stretched his back over the back of the bench, forming an arch, his glass upright between his hands. He shut his eyes.

Anita sipped the whisky. 'Barney does the full-on family thing,' she said.

Mark was silent – as was the house behind them. It had ceased to make noises. Late-night gurgles in cisterns, water in downpipes, creaks, and then the fabric itself had sighed and settled. She guessed the upstairs lights were all out.

'Say something nice to me. I need encouragement,' Mark said.

'What sort of thing? I do wish you'd sit up.'

'That I'm not worthless.'

She sighed.

'Mother sighs. You remind me of her sometimes. Ruthless.'

'She adores you. Mark and Barney. She's always said that. Although you're younger.'

He righted himself. 'Well, it sounds better.'

She suggested they move further down the garden, out of earshot of the house. So, after Mark had fetched the bottle of whisky from indoors, they went to sit on the bench at the far end of the lawn.

At one o'clock they were still out there – drinking. There was no flow to what they said. They stopped and started again – often prompted by a question from Anita. She could cope with that. She didn't require balance.

Mark was subdued. He remained in the other place – wherever that was – that had a bad feel to it. Consciousness – never a clear pane of glass – had become contaminated. Anita did cloudy, every shade from pale to murky, but that was all right. She was at home in dim light.

Mark's stories had dried up – along with his interest in the past. Anita asked him where he had been lately. He travelled to the Gulf States and Asia for work. He mentioned some of the places. Flashes of brightly lit interiors came to her: offices, airports, hotels. In the peace of the dark garden she saw the security check-in; her brother stepping through the electronic portal, his shoes and his belt off, his hands loose at his sides.

She was flattered he was talking to her, though he wasn't telling her anything she hadn't already heard from Veronica. It was all quite mundane.

Their glasses were empty and stood abandoned on the grass at their feet. Mark moved on to the hip flask and took regular swigs from it. He went indoors for a refill and returned, walking steadily – though with overprecision – watching his step in the dark. He sat down again. They continued to talk. Mark drank. The silences grew longer.

'Do I look awful?' Anita asked, peering at her watch.

He turned his head to look at her. His focus was somewhere over her shoulder.

'You look lovely,' he said, with several seconds' delay, like a telephone with faulty transmission.

'We're tired,' she said. 'We should go in.'

She stood up and put her hand out to him. He leant forward, getting his balance, took the hand and got to his feet.

The house represented Saturday. Tall and old; supportive of marriage. By getting up and going towards it, they would be closing the gap between night and morning, bringing the day closer.

'Let's see each other in London,' she said, though he wouldn't remember a thing.

He fumbled in his pocket, checking for the hip flask.

'It's all right, Mark. You've got it.' She repositioned his hand, tucking his arm inside hers. 'Lean on me, if you like.'

She took a step; then he took one. He could walk.

'We don't have to run on single tracks, do we? I mean we could meet up. Just sometimes. I wouldn't barge in on your social life. We could go and watch cormorants. I get your news from Mum. But you could tell me.' She would say all this again when he was sober.

The flowers in the border were inert and mysterious. At this time of night, they had a vegetative life of their own. The pale ones gave off night scents, like signals.

'Do you remember the summer Nick Halsey came?' she said.

'Who?' Mark said, stumbling.

They reached the house. The lamp was still on in the hall. Anita guided him in through the door. Maybe changing location had had a bracing effect. He seemed a bit less out of it.

'Wait there,' she whispered, jamming his hand on the newel post at the bottom of the stairs. 'I'm going to get some water.'

'Bed,' he said, loudly. 'Need bed.'

'Sh.' She caught sight of them both in the mirror. 'Jesus.'

It was too late for water. She wouldn't get him to

drink it. A sofa seemed a better idea than the stairs. But he had already begun the ascent, hand over hand on the banister rail, with his back angled forward, as though he were about to start crawling.

'Hang on, Mark, I'm behind you.'

She kept a grip on him. He pressed on. One flight. Some trouble at the first landing when he continued upwards, expecting more stairs. His foot thudded on nothingness.

'It's the landing,' she hissed. 'Walk. Turn.'

He staggered on the level; all over the place. He was better on stairs. How bizarre. She foresaw the next landing, got a foot on his foot and stopped him from phantom climbing.

One more flight. Same manoeuvre. They were home. Barney's bedroom door was shut. Mark's ajar. She propelled him through it and on to the bed; a dead weight. He lay spreadeagled. She took off one shoe, then the other. There was a hole in the sock at the heel. She left him and went to the bathroom to get some water.

When she returned with the toothbrush mug he had shifted. His head was on one side, an arm flung over his body. She opened the sash window wide at the top and closed the curtains.

'There's some water, if you need it,' she said. 'On your table.'

He grunted.

'Sleep tight. See you in the morning.'

She went out and closed the door quietly. Two doors shut. Two brothers. She needed to get to bed herself. Mark would have a hangover. So would she. They wouldn't be the first in the history of weddings.

She glimpsed a way of being in the family. If not admired, she could conceivably be valued as someone who – who what? She stumbled over that part, confused between roles. A childish element in her rejoiced at the flaw that had cropped up in Mark. She was his friend, wasn't she? And Veronica had chosen her, if temporarily, as his keeper. She would be a kind of bridge between her mother and her brother. A dependable link. Would that be good enough?

At around half past three in the morning, she woke up. Her mouth was dry. She walked along to the bathroom and failed to notice her brother on the landing, although she saw him on the way back – and afterwards, imprinted. She drank copious amounts. She cupped her hands and drank as though from a fountain, splashing water everywhere.

4

After her collapse at the kitchen table, Anita slept, on and off, through Friday and Saturday, in a hollow, dreamless sleep. She missed Barney's second wedding entirely. When she woke she felt as tired as if she had run a race. She had a strange, metallic taste in her mouth which she associated with the chemical smell of The Hesperia. Drifting off again, she seemed to hear the swish of a broom. She thought she was back in Laurence's ground-floor apartment.

The shapes of furniture in the room settled into a recognised pattern. Chest of drawers, cupboard, desk under the window. The bed she was in was single; on the table next to it, a glass of water. Anita moved the pillow and settled her head on the cool of the sheet and went back to sleep.

At around midday, she woke again, eased herself from the duvet and put her bare feet on the rug. Her neck ached. She circled her head slowly to release it. Outside in the garden, men called to each other. She heard bangs and crashes, the scraping of metal on metal. The racket seemed part of some general catastrophe. She couldn't bear to look out. Then she remembered the tent. It was being dismantled. Did that mean it was Monday already? She hadn't set foot in it.

The walls had been repainted a strange lemony colour. She felt disconnected from the girl who had inhabited the room. Only one male had ever got into the bed: Jonathan Zeals, a melancholy eighteen-year-old with long white legs, whose parents lived in Bishop's Waltham. Gavin had never come near – which relieved her of one set of memories.

She missed the usual paraphernalia she spread about: make-up, hairdryer, paperbacks, shoes. Her overnight bag stood in the middle of the floor, zipped up. She raised herself to standing and retied the pyjama trousers that had shifted off-centre. Unsteady and rocking, as from a boat trip, she went across to the cupboard and found the clothes she had arrived in, hanging up on a faded satin-covered coat hanger.

She opened the bedroom door and walked along the passage. The bathroom was cold and echoey and smelled of eau de cologne soap. She ran a bath and climbed in while the water was running, letting the gush of hot and trickle of cold mingle round her feet. In between the two taps was a slick of green limescale. She lay without thinking. The voices and banging continued.

Submerged, she noticed that the sounds outside moved around the garden as in a box; up and down, side to side. She became warm and then chilled again and got out to dry herself.

Back in the bedroom, she scrabbled ineffectively in the overnight bag. The various dresses she might have worn for the wedding were rolled in flimsy balls. Underneath was the ordinary stuff that she needed: knickers, spare T-shirts, extra jumper, socks. Everything happened abruptly; the different stages of dressing, all demarcated. She had, for the time being, lost the flow that allowed her to think and do simultaneously and felt a kind of homesickness, not for a particular place but for habit that smoothed the path from one action to the next.

Half-dressed, she went over to the mirror. Her face was winter pale and faintly mottled. She could emerge wrecked, or make an effort. Dipping fingers into a pot of moisturiser, she rubbed circles on her skin. This, she guessed was the easy part. She made up her eyes – smoky lines across the upper lid, dragged and extended. Over-extended; like the wrong length of curtain rail. She spiked up her hair. Her fingers poked through the tufts like antennae. The effect was odder than usual. The mirror was unprepared for her, as if it had lost the habit of reflecting. She tried smiling and not smiling but the lack of recognition persisted. Revisiting the make-up bag she identified mascara, blusher and lipgloss – and applied them. When she had finished she sat on the white painted chair.

5

'Feeling better, Anita?' Howard asked, coming into the kitchen. 'Good,' he said before the nod was complete.

He stood and looked out of the window at the men at work on the tent, his hands in the pockets of his trousers. 'They'll soon have it down.'

After a few minutes, he turned round. 'How was Bulgaria? Did you see anything of the Thracian tombs?'

The slight droop to his left eye was pronounced.

Anita switched on the kettle. Loose pieces of limescale began to rattle in the bottom.

'No,' she said.

'Herodotus claimed that if the Thracians hadn't fallen out amongst themselves they would have been the most powerful civilisation of the day. They had gold.'

'Is it Monday?' she asked.

'Monday? No. Still Sunday.'

Howard, with lines of concentration between his eyebrows, continued to talk about Thrace. The half-remembered facts were a comfort to him and, she suspected, intended as a distraction to her. The voice was monotonous with a suggestion of authority and reason. She heard the gobbets of history, retrieved from his youth, without properly listening, and wanted to help, though she couldn't; only hoped that she wouldn't say or do anything to disturb him. It was unlikely at this stage that there would be a breakthrough of communication. The thought of the effort required to alter a lifetime's pattern was itself laborious. She wasn't up for it – not at her best – and had to acknowledge that even when she had been – more at her best – she had taken the easy course. They had been glad, after Mark's death and the years of bereavement that followed, to settle for the doable. They couldn't rise above that.

The water that came out of the kettle was flecked with pale shards that sank on top of the tea bag. Anita let the liquid brew and settle, then added a slug of milk. What resulted looked disgusting and she tipped it down the sink.

'Something wrong with the tea?' Howard broke off from his disquisition to ask.

'I didn't put enough water in the kettle. My fault,' she said.

He hovered behind her. Had it been lunchtime or evening he would have offered her a drink and that would have been easier. He would have headed to the pantry and chosen a bottle, gone through the distracting ritual of checking the label, uncorking and sniffing, getting out suitable wine glasses. Fortified, she might have asked about the wedding. He would have picked out one or two moments that he remembered. Something someone had said that seemed interesting. They wouldn't exactly have *chatted*.

He hung a few feet away while she upended the kettle over the sink, letting the loose pieces of limescale fall out; jiggling it to and fro, to dislodge the flakes that were stuck. He looked on anxiously. She hadn't done this before. No one had, over the years. He hadn't known that the kettle harboured strange matter. The noise it made every morning – the rattling like hailstones on a roof – that was surely what happened with boiling. Here was his youngest child who had no instinct for putting things to rights – rather the contrary – shaking a household object and unfixing its innards. No good came from meddling. The free play of the mind, the right to roam mentally; this was what he believed in. The rest should stay fixed or be dealt with by professionals. Hadn't Anita once interfered with a mirror? Taken it down from the wall on the upstairs landing? Some damn fool nonsense that ended with the chain being damaged, which would never have happened had it remained in its place.

Anita guessed her father's thoughts. He had referred to the mishandling of the mirror on more than one occasion. There was something hapless about her which she knew undermined him.

Outside in the garden, the tent was coming down, pole by pole. The men moved in an orderly dance. Already the view was partially restored; the curve of the lawn round the Indian bean tree emerged.

Anita refilled the kettle. The kitchen was suspiciously scrubbed; its surfaces clear. The piles of newspapers and documents in brown envelopes that usually took up one end of the long table had vanished along with the stack of papers that tottered in the corner of the dresser.

'It looks very tidy,' she said.

'That was for the caterers. They needed space. Bits of boys and girls; uniformed up. Very well organised. Couldn't fault them.'

'Where's it gone then, all the stuff?'

'Ronny put it somewhere. Moved it. Mostly hers, you know.'

6

Barney and Harriet's wedding in Berkshire had gone ahead, as planned. There was still a chance at that stage. They kept going on hope and adrenalin. Veronica and Howard stayed by Mark who was wired up in the high-dependency unit of Southampton University Hospital. Veronica insisted that Anita attend the wedding and represent the family. She said she or Howard would put in an appearance if they had the opportunity. Barney and Harriet wanted to postpone but the day rolled on like a train keeping to a Swiss timetable.

Anita's fear of the wedding somehow wasn't swallowed up by the greater trouble. Cars converged on the village near Newbury; expensive catafalques of metal with their tops glinting in the sunshine. They glided into that English place and, in a sudden disorder of wheels on kerbs and hasty parking, came to a halt within walking distance of a church tower. One by one, bodies spilled out and stood upright. They raised their arms to adjust waistcoats or pat stained-glass-coloured hats. It was a Last Judgement scene and the news, as it got round, just as mixed.

The friends and relatives rose to the occasion. So many weddings in a lifetime but this was one to recall. The singing was lustier, the reds and blues brighter. Sound came and went, as in an echo chamber; resonant then hushed. Paper rustled. The congregation joined in the responses:

O Lord, send them help from thy holy place;
And evermore defend them.
Be unto them a tower of strength,
From the face of their enemy.
O Lord, hear our prayer;
And let our cry come unto thee.

The words, beautiful as the shipping forecast and as mysterious, united them. They *were* in the same boat but had been spared – for the moment.

Anita, with a mind full of shocking images, tried to be inconspicuous. At least, after the terrible night, she had an excuse for looking haggard. In her flimsiest, sexiest frock, stitched from feathery pieces, she found herself dependent on a black shawl for decency. Her hair, dyed too dark for her pale face, was tied back in a knot. Far from merging, she knew she stood out; an eye-catching, inappropriate shadow.

The wedding photographer was allowed a few shots of Barney and Harriet and despatched. Anita got in a car with some friends of the Mostyns to travel the short distance to Harriet's parents' house. Granny Randall was already sitting in the back, strapped in with her bag squared up on her knees. She clasped Anita's hand in her elegant, veiny one. They went over the road bumps, bouncing on the leather seats, and drove on through the Berkshire village, passing a convenience store, a hairdressing salon, a shop selling country casuals. They paused at two pedestrian crossings about fifty metres apart from each other; the stripes that had once been white were faded and mottled by tyre marks. People were out doing Saturday-afternoon shopping. Granny told stories of Mark as a child. The couple, whoever they were, listened and sometimes murmured respectfully. Anita saw only their backs; one bald head, one in a high crowned hat decorated with a grey cockade that spurted like a firework from the ribbon whenever the wheels went over a bump.

Granny's precise voice continued; her old-fashioned enunciation perfectly formed for tales of prep school and long-ago Christmases. The couple, perhaps, would have liked to hear more about the accident. It would be something to talk about on their homeward journey. The timing – there was always some element of timing in an accident – the minutes either way that would have made a difference – and the miscalculation. It wasn't useful to

215

talk about blame, but, if one could whittle it out – in the nicest possible way – error generally came into the picture.

Granny persisted with her monologue through a less agreeable part of the village – boarded-up, red-brick premises, a garage forecourt that had lost its pumps, a sign saying 'Station' – and out again, past sugar-almond-coloured cottages with hanging baskets.

Anita marvelled at her grandmother: the impeccable defence system that would take them to the front door of this unknown house and beyond. Storytelling – superior to mere speculation – protected them. Summers of grey-grained garden chairs were evoked; striped grasses down by the stream, where Mark and Barney used to hide. He seemed to be listening; the taut, lively boy who crouched, ready to spring. 'I wonder where Mark's gone?' They had to say it loudly enough for him to hear them. Sometimes he took his great-grand-father's stick from the umbrella stand in the hall and pretended to go rock climbing up the stairs. As Granny used the forbidden word, Anita saw the cockade quiver like an antenna that picked up a signal. If Granny noticed, she showed no sign and powered onwards. 'I might not be back for supper,' Mark told them. He was splendid but normal. The best possible boy. Not all plain sailing, of course. Those terrifying breath-holding episodes. He would yell a continuous, head-quivering yell, until his lungs were empty. Then, failing to breathe in again, his lips would go blue. Veronica did anything to avoid those incidents. She gave in to him too soon. Mark never lost consciousness.

Granny had bypassed Anita, was getting earlier and earlier. Anita, wired tight as a gut string, gazed into the faraway time of her pre-existence; not billed as paradise – perfectly ordinary. Anita could be kind about that era; unconflicted. She tried to hold on to it. The same with her mother. The little girl in an embroidered smock, standing on the top step of Granny and Grandpa Randall's house in Glebe Place. She could be kind about her too.

As the wheels turned into a drive, Granny cleared her throat to begin thanking. She steadied the bag and held tight to her granddaughter's hand. They were delivered.

The crisis was drawn out. Barney's wedding came and went. The honeymoon was cancelled. Mark was moved from the high-dependency unit in the hospital to Rayley Park Clinic. He was stable. Veronica cut down her hours but carried on working. Howard took refuge in the office. When home, he shut the door of his study and listened to Mozart operas.

217

Mark had a birthday at Rayley Park Clinic. The previous year, for his thirtieth, he had been in The Fat Duck at Bray, enjoying Sunday lunch with friends and family. Some of the same people who had celebrated with him visited the clinic: Veronica and Howard, Barney and Harriet, Anita, Simon Hyde-Johnson, Evadne Stark, Dee Bringhurst, Simon Sigrist.

There was still hope at that stage. The approximate time in which the Earth makes its revolution round the sun was believed to be a period in which recovery was possible. Even the medics went by the Earth's orbit. The chances diminished over the twelve months but that didn't stop anyone from fastening on a date. Until then was temporary; and afterwards, permanent.

Only Veronica refrained from believing in a fairy-tale cut-off point. Hope was either at the bottom of the jar or it wasn't. In her restrained way, she steered clear of stories of dramatic recovery. They seemed to her strangely vulgar; nothing to do with Mark. And, as far as Veronica was concerned, though Granny Randall prayed daily, neither prayer nor God made a difference to the outcome, since they operated – or not – either way. She raised her eyebrows at excessive sentiment.

She was hard to gainsay. No one found a weak corner in her that could be loosened and tugged. Tall and angular, with her patrician nose and stiff wavy hair, she looked totally sane, and her voice, on the gruff side, signalled rationality and a sound education.

Mark underwent the birthday and other days. He had a beautiful face, good bones, his mother's nose, dark lashes. If his head was moved by the nurse who came to turn him, he opened or closed his eyes like a doll. On the birthday morning, Howard said what he always said; that birthdays didn't count after the age of twelve. He could have said something different but he stuck to the formula. He patted his wife's shoulder and told her that he would try to call in at Rayley Park after work.

7

When Howard left the kitchen Anita felt herself slipping. She noticed, for the first time, a radio, left on in the garden. It played to no one. The tent men were loading up the lorry. Percussive noises of metal on metal, shouts and clatters, now came – at lower volume – from the front of the house. Without her father – correctly dressed but without a tie and smelling of morning soap – the room began to tilt. Oblique reflections, as if caused by the refraction of two sets of glass, cut chunks out of the objects around her and turned them into configurations painted by a Cubist artist. The tea tin, the toaster, the kettle, the bottle of washing-up liquid – were all distorted. She hadn't eaten – must eat. They – a doctor – might have dosed her with something. Diazepam? The bitter after-taste in her mouth indicated some kind of medication, though she associated it with the smell of The Hesperia. Her senses were merging. She recalled the glass of water by her bed but no pill bottle. There wouldn't have been, would there? They would have put it out of reach; out of harm's way. She couldn't remember a doctor.

She had gone haywire after Mark's death. She was bundled home to Elvham, then, briefly, into hospital.

'You have a history of drug-taking,' the newly qualified doctor had said, gazing at her notes on screen and referring to the something and nothing of leisure time with Gavin that Anita should have disavowed categorically.

'Well, I have now,' Anita replied. 'Or are antipsychotics a kind of biscuit?'

She recalled the ordeal as a place, or rather several disconnected places that she viewed in close-up. The images that had led to the psychiatric unit were still present; colourfast in her system.

She carried on breathing and kept close to some unnamed centre. She hoped to avoid a splintering.

She had always craved safety, and had tried to achieve it, when she wasn't being wimpish, by making a rush in the opposite direction: sabotaging her schooling, living with Gav – in a minor way, taking up Laurence's offer and running away to the Black Sea.

Her mother had told her to be her brother's keeper for a few hours but she had known better. Other people noticed her lack of judgement. Even Gav – from the stronghold of self-conviction – had remarked on it. 'You *knew* what I was like, Anita. I haven't changed.' And perhaps her fault was that having made a dash into danger, her nerve failed her. She was never the bold one.

221

Anita was still angry – angry and disbelieving – that, nine years on, the family had gone for a reprise of Barney's first wedding. The same format, the same guests on the groom's side, give or take a few deaths; only the location and the time of year were different – and the name of the bride. It was, she thought, a kind of obstinacy but also pride. The Mostyns and Randalls were the sort of people of whom it is said, 'If they got through *that* then surely we can get through *this*.' Except, they hadn't got through it. Barney's marriage to Harriet had failed – and her relationship with Gavin. Gav left for good soon after her breakdown. Veronica and Howard purchased the Chelsea flat she and Gavin had rented. They stood firm.

Had Anita been present at the second wedding, she might have heard murmurs of admiration among the guests at the family's fortitude. The friends were dogged and cut from the same English cloth. Schooling, property, the form of things – nothing altered their preoccupations. Anita's mistake was to expect that her parents might change. The tragedy of Mark's death had entrenched them; the old ways of behaving were turned into props.

Veronica was a husk, compared with what she had been; powerless. She was growing old and heaven knew what kinds of fears assailed her. The misaligned buttons, the foundation cream sometimes wonkily applied; these had always been part of her mother – the favouring of intellect over appearance. Yet now she took more trouble; spent longer in front of the mirror, checking. The put-downs, too – those quick ripostes Veronica had made in exactly the same way, a million times – she, herself, seemed to tire of them. If you caught her eye when she was in mid-flow, she looked back defiantly; conveying that if other people would stop being such bloody fools, she could stop this panjandrumming. All the same, Anita didn't quite believe in the husk.

Unsteadily, hand over hand, Anita made her way round the kitchen towards the bread bin, which turned out to be full of small, shiny, bomb-shaped rolls. No doubt the fridge and freezer were also stacked with leftovers from the reception. She picked a roll and put one end to her mouth, cautiously. It was dry and chewy. She made herself eat it. Then switched on the newly disencumbered kettle.

When she thought about the lost time between the wedding-rehearsal tea on Thursday and waking up that Sunday morning, she recalled only sleep, drawn curtains, the refuge under the duvet. She was sure no doctor had visited. Veronica was on good terms with her GP, Beth Wright. Beth's four children were all successful lawyers and doctors. She kept her prescription pad in her bag. It was not impossible that Veronica had asked her for 'something'.

While the kettle came to the boil calmly, without

jittering, Anita opened kitchen cupboards. Sometimes medicines found their way into them. Cough linctus, tasting of tar, and the blister pack of Disprin. Halves for the young, as her mother had had no truck with junior versions of medicines. She would like to find the diazepam.

'Has that old Peugeot finally died?' Veronica asked when Anita talked about ringing up for a cab to take her to the station. 'I noticed you didn't come in it.'

They were sitting in the drawing room. A fire had been lit. Saxon slept; flat as he could make himself, all four legs stretched towards the heat. It was his best impression of a cut-out. Howard was reading the *Financial Times* from the previous day, salvaging the Saturday that had been lost to the wedding. His half-moon glasses rested down his nose. Every now and then, he reached out, under the lamp, for the cup of tea that was empty.

Having had an afternoon rest, Anita felt a little steadier. She shook her head in reply to her mother. 'It's not quite kaput and when it is I won't replace it.'

'You can't afford to, I suppose?' Veronica said.

'That too.'

'Did you get *anything* out of the trip to Bulgaria?'

224

Anita picked up the mobile that was lying beside her on the sofa and scrolled through the address book. E for Emerald Cabs. An old entry and not entirely reliable – the cab firm, that is. The number was fine; it kept on ringing with the ancient-sounding warble that suggested the phone at the other end had a heavy Bakelite handset and an alpha-numeric dial. She had never understood how some numbers were trapped in a time warp.

'Are they not answering?' Veronica asked.

'No. It is Sunday. They might not be there,' Anita said.

'I'll run you to the station if you insist on leaving but I do wish you'd stay the night. The travel will be dismal. And we've got so much food left over. The fridge is bursting,' Veronica said.

Howard looked up. 'No, don't go, Netta.'

When the clock's hands pointed to half past five, Veronica suggested to Howard that it was time for a drink.

There was recognition in the word 'dismal'. Her mother wished to spare her the desolation of Southern Railway on an off night – though other less simple depredations Anita hadn't been spared. She waited half an hour and tried Emerald Cabs again. This time she hung up sooner.

At seven, they decided on an early supper. Veronica

was in favour of a buffet, so they took it in turns to go to the fridge. The rolls came out of the bread bin. They each returned to the drawing room with an individual portion of salmon mousse, a knife and a plate.

'I'm looking forward to that Eton mess,' Howard said. 'It was awfully good.'

8

Anita had no idea how to be. 'Don't go so often. What good does it do?' Fran used to say. 'Look after *you*.' It was easy to dole out advice. Anita wondered where Mark was. His essence, life force, soul – whatever you called it – had to be somewhere. She tried to imagine it hovering over the hospital bed, like a guardian angel or a bubble thought in a comic. She felt his spirit had gone, or, at best, was trapped inside – a dried-up bean, a tiny world folded in on itself, waiting for water and light. She raided the Internet, opening ever more distant pages; stories, mostly from small towns in America, where the comatose woke and said, 'Mom.' She flicked through improbable accounts, in a trance. Hours passed. She tried online psychic readings. The more sophisticated 'remotes' required a credit card. She ventured into a strange tunnel of prediction and became claustrophobic. Such sampling would have struck Veronica and Howard as vulgar. Anita never mentioned her research but she couldn't help feeling that English pragmatism stood in the way of miracle, or even a wild card of good luck.

Rayley Park Clinic, near Woking, was at the end of a drive that curved through rhododendron bushes. 'Park' was inaccurate; there had never been a park, just a large garden. A shrubbery lay between the gates and the house. There was a rectangular lawn, stamped with rose borders, and beyond, a disused tennis court. Chimney pots and the top of the front gable were visible from the road, but approaching through the dull-leaved evergreens, all sight of the building vanished. It sat in a hollow, secluded and smug. The original house, built in the 1890s, had been added to a century later and was flanked on either side by two rectangular blocks in approximately matching brick; Sidney Wing and Josephine Wing, named after the first owners. Had Colonel and Mrs Spalding returned from the dead, they would have been surprised by the familiar nomenclature, also by the inside of their house that – apart from fire doors – ran seamlessly on three floors from one end of Sidney to the other end of Josephine. Access between floors was provided by lifts and functional stairways. Behind the facade, all that remained of the old house was the morning room to the right of the entrance, and that was unnervingly intact; a Victorian box, complete with fireplace, black marble surround, picture rail and mouldings. Called the 'Visitors' Room', it lacked the Spaldings' dust-trapping knick-knacks but new clutter had been supplied or

228

donated: back copies of *Country Life*, calming books with the words 'eternal' or 'reflections' in the titles, Scrabble to pass the time, framed photographs of local dignitaries shaking hands with the staff. Sofas and chairs, upholstered in hard-wearing fabric, were grouped around the hearth. An arrangement of silk flowers in a large pottery jug stood on the fireplace tiles. Radiators, tucked under the windows, were concealed behind latticed covers.

Veronica, chatting to Gabrielle at the reception desk, said Howard had a dinner to go to, he wouldn't be coming.

'Oh, we have one visitor.' Gabrielle enjoyed a hint of suspense.

The door of the Visitors' Room was ajar.

'Really?' Veronica said.

'She hasn't gone upstairs yet. She's making herself a coffee,' Gabrielle said. 'I knew you'd be pleased.'

Anita, hearing the exchange, reboiled the water in the kettle. The side table was laid with stacked cups and saucers and bowls containing a selection of tea bags, coffee, sugar in wraps and tiny cartons of long-life milk. They were replenished daily – but it seemed to Anita that they were an unchanging collection. The alternative options were stuck at the back – four sachets of peppermint, four of camomile, two of Well-Being – for those who were prepared to risk disappointment. She stuck to

229

the instant coffee. With a wrap of brown sugar added, the taste reminded her of childhood visits to her grand-parents. She sprinkled the granules into the cup and poured on the hot water and was adding the sugar – about to smell the comforting smell – when her mother came into the room. Anita immediately turned and went towards Veronica who was approaching with her loping, slightly clumsy walk. A bunch of late roses from the garden poked out of the top of the basket she was carrying. The face, with its messages – the extreme tension in the muscles around the jaw, the distraction in the eyes – came closer and closer. The two women embraced. Anita felt her mother's rings pressing into her back, through the lightweight cloth of her shirt.

Veronica turned away. She picked a hair from the lapel of her jacket. She asked about Anita's journey and her day in the Islington gallery that sold contemporary ceramics. 'How's the pot shop?' she enquired.

Anita, unable to be herself – locked into not being herself – hoped for spontaneity that never came. Instead, she played the part of being natural.

The evening sun shone through the bay window.

'Shall we go up?' Veronica said.

Anita followed her out of the door and across the reception area. Gabrielle was absent from the desk. The red light on the telephone was winking, indicating that a caller was leaving a message. They went into Sidney Wing. The monitor over the lift showed a continuous broken line. Veronica pressed the button and the doors slid apart. They stepped into the space that was roomy for two people – large enough for a hospital bed. Anita knew the grey-speckled interior, the bright downlighters with rainbow auras, the closed-in smell; they were imprinted on her mind. At the second floor, they got out. They turned right and walked along the corridor. The doors, symmetrically arranged, were all ajar. Daylight ran in bands across the carpet.

'Gabrielle has changed to evenings, because of her morning sickness,' Veronica said. 'They've binned off that rather wild-looking man from the agency. I can't say I'm sorry. I wasn't too bad – though smells could set me off. Harrods I remember was particularly difficult – the mixture of scent and lunch.' She began putting the roses in a vase. She chopped the ends with scissors and arranged them in the glass jug that had a blurry ring halfway down, caused by hard water.

The room was a decent-sized box. The window, framed with discreetly patterned curtains that stopped at the sill, looked out over a single horse chestnut tree, currently heavy with spiky green fruit. There were three upright chairs with arms, a washbasin, a chest of drawers, a special hospital bed.

Anita had never got used to the way her mother carried on a conversation in Sidney Wing, as if she were at home, or in the car. Her own ability to chatter on faltered. She made herself small in one of the chairs and remained silent. She practised something that resembled meditation but probably wasn't because being in a state of it felt pointless and sinister and continued to be so however long it went on. She chose a piece of wall above the chest of drawers that she could stare at without moving her head. Her eyes rested there. She was easily distracted by the window.

Silence wasn't an option. To talk was necessary; talking *to* Mark, as well as among themselves.

'*Can* he hear?' Anita had once asked one of the nurses when her mother was out of earshot.

'Oh, *yes*,' the nurse replied. 'And if he can't, well at least we're trying.'

But Anita had been unable to extemporise. She lacked some ordinary human quality that the others possessed. Spontaneity – which she had thought she had – deserted her. Her level of inhibition went soaring off the scale. Thinking of what to say and forcing herself to speak, she felt as if she were being asked to perform a sexual act she couldn't stomach.

The visits were easier when Howard was there. He brandished a newspaper and brought the outside with him in the volume of his greeting. He had a good carrying voice, suited to fresh-air games like croquet and hailing cabs in London. He paced about for a while, told the room at large the cricket scores, then plucked at the knees of his trousers and settled in a chair with the *Financial Times*, or a set of board papers. From time to time, he looked at the two women over the top of his half-moon glasses or replied to Veronica. Anita admired the way that both her parents made a kind of home for themselves at Rayley Park, though it was a scaled-down version – and a parody of the real life they led. It was as if they played house in that small room: stay-at-home wife, in charge of all things domestic; working husband, who blew in from the City. In the centre was the beloved, breathing, sleeping child who would grasp your fingers if you placed them in his hand.

A knock at the door, though it was open. A courtesy knock. It was one of the nurses, Fernanda, with her hair pulled back tight from her shiny forehead and fastened by a silk flower. Anita began to push her chair away from the bed.

'Please. No need to move. I turn with you there.' Fernanda squeezed past.

Veronica smiled. 'You always make it look so easy, Fernanda, though you're such a little thing.'

9

Barney was travelling a lot at the time, making frequent journeys across the Atlantic. Harriet also worked long hours. Their free time was limited but they fitted in weekends in Hampshire. Occasionally, one or other would accompany Veronica and Howard to the clinic. The tension eased on these occasions. Veronica seemed to relax. Howard emerged from his study. Harriet was charming and natural with the Mostyns. She talked about work and improvements that she and Barney were making to their flat in Brook Green. She spoke of the wedding as if it were a lovely, isolated event and asked after people she had been introduced to, matching them up with their presents. Veronica went along with all this. She talked at speed in a voice that carried over the walls of the garden. She appraised the friends; their career moves, successes and failures. So-and-so was 'highly intelligent'. Harriet nodded, her face open and receptive. Veronica's requirements were stringent but once you were in, you were in.

They sat in the garden. It was a good summer that

year; sunny by day with light rain at night. Nobody wanted to be indoors. They ate lunch outside. Veronica's *salade composée* consisted of lettuce, cold potato and other fridge leftovers, sometimes with a tin of something fishy thrown in. Harriet said, 'How delicious.'

Anita ate almost nothing. She saw the garden table, laid for lunch, as though through thick glass. She assumed it was the same for her parents and brother, that they were each trapped in an individual vessel of pain, though theirs allowed them to carry on talking and eating. She missed Viking; the friendly presence that flopped down in sun or shade. Having lost purpose herself, she felt the lack of a being with strong wishes. A child would have done, but she was used to Viking with his chestnut-coloured eyes; the one who chased bluebottles and padded after her into the kitchen.

Kingsfold House, at least from the outside, was non-committal; Mark's old window, an unblinking eye. Anita was bothered by the lack of signals. In a crisis, the house had nothing to offer; having been, it seemed, no more than a building all along. The interior was different; a maze of associations she had yet to find a path through.

In the garden, crickets chirped in the long grasses down by the stream, vying with bees that buzzed in the border. The roses flourished. There was one dud among them, an anonymous rambler that predated the Mostyns. The roots were deep and ran under the south wall; its woody stems had got into the peach tree. Year after year, it produced blooms that fattened but failed to open. 'Needs digging up,' Howard said, every June, but nothing was done. That summer, petals the colour of old linen unfolded. No browning, no fused blooms with squishy middles. The scent was mild with a greenish note. Its time had come, though it still lacked a name.

The family had never been so much together. It was a strange togetherness that no one knew how to handle. Howard, who normally craved solitude, invented little projects – cutting back a viburnum that was making too much shade, sorting out the shed, making the larder window squirrel-proof. He suggested these tentatively, as if, during an outbreak of measles, he had been made deputy form prefect. Veronica was taken aback but, in a new, tired way, failed to oppose him. Both he and Veronica looked older. They paid less attention to standing up straight. Howard's left eye drooped further and Veronica, in her grief, had turned against the hairdresser. Grey spread from the roots of her hair.

Howard's projects were the strategy of an elderly man; it was as if he feared that, unless the young ones were kept occupied, they would leave prematurely. Harriet and Barney entered into the spirit of the thing. They piled up branches for a bonfire, or got out the stepladder

– whatever it happened to be. They were glad of something to do. The task on one occasion was to 'go through the books' – real books that had been piled in the summer house since Howard's father's death. Their spines were bleached paler than their front and back covers. They had been waiting twenty years for a purge.

Removing the cartons of books from the summer house and bringing them on to the lawn into the full light of day was hard work but Howard insisted. Anita watched spiders run out from the deckchair frames. Her father said that as long as the books stayed in the summer house he would never deal with them. The pile of rejections grew higher – soon it was several piles. Set against the lively green of the grass, the books had no appeal and no sentimental value, until you opened them and saw names and dates, handwritten in ink that had faded – or pieces of thin paper, stuck in with brown glue. *Prize for Latin awarded to Barnabus Percival Mostyn.* It was better to be a plant that sprouted, flourished, and went to sleep again all within the year. The dust was carried away on the air. Anita saw something savage in the process. A second burial of someone – her Mostyn grandfather – who had lived out his lifespan and not lost a child.

'Take any you like, my dear,' Howard said, addressing Harriet who was sitting on the grass, leafing through a book about Roald Amundsen.

Veronica leant over, peering in the boxes. 'Don't say that, Howard. It puts pressure on. If Harriet takes the book, it will only be to keep *you* happy. It'll end up in the charity shop just the same,' she said. 'And *they'll* probably bin most of them.'

Howard turned his head to the sun and closed his eyes. He had joined in the heavy work and now he was taking a rest. The old masculine topics – cricket, aeronautics, exploration, war, chess – and the chaps who excelled in them – their biographies and memoirs bound in discoloured cloth and pepped up with black and white photographs and fold-out maps – they were all for the chop. B.P., while alive, represented his books – drawing spirit from matter. His dead heroes had lived on in him. When the spring clean was complete they would be gone.

Separated from the others by a barrier of packing cartons, Anita turned over pages.

'What's gripping you, Anita?' Veronica asked.

Anita finished the sentence she was reading. '*Old Flying Days*,' she said.

'And is it interesting?'

'Mr Flying Days sounds happy. It's a world without wives and girlfriends,' Anita replied. 'The men get into their contraptions and sail up over Hendon.'

She had left Gav behind in London. For all she knew,

he was sky-writing, 'Goodbye, Anita.' He seemed far, far away.

Once the books had been boxed up and placed in the hall for transporting there was a lull. Talking stopped. Harriet and Barney lay on a blanket on the grass and read different sections of the Sunday newspapers. From time to time, Barney put out a hand and stroked Harriet's buttocks. Veronica walked by the flower border. She snipped wayward shoots with the secateurs. Sitting on the bench, Howard woke from his nap and gazed stolidly into the distance. Anita went down to the stream, to wash off the musty smell of the books. She knelt on bare knees and trailed her hands through water.

10

On her first morning back at work, Anita arrived half an hour early, having lost the knack of cutting it fine. She had been away for four weeks; the first one spent partly in Bulgaria. At Green Park, where she came out of the tube, a white mist hung over the grass. Trees and benches were suspended and rootless. She took in gulps of frozen air as she waited for the lights to change and bring the flow of Piccadilly traffic to a stop.

Having crossed the road, she entered White Horse Street with its dungeon-like walls and emerged in an empty Shepherd Market. The swish of the road sweeper's broom on damp pavements interrupted a dead calm. The place yawned – more from boredom than weariness, though late waking was deep in its bones. Tiny cafés, tucked in passageways, were built for slow starts and recovery – not coffee to go. She headed for Vesuvio. She always went there. The café had a bow window that deserved a sea view but looked straight into the neighbouring Lebanese restaurant a couple of metres away. The premises were so close to each other that at

240

midday when the lamps came on you could see what people were eating and lip-read their conversations. The sun never penetrated. In summer, tables with white cloths were squeezed into the long narrow shadow between the buildings.

Anita wriggled along a red leatherette seat with a fixed shelf of Formica in front of it and ordered an espresso. She was the only customer.

As soon as the coffee machine stopped its explosions, the waiter addressed her. 'You been away? On 'oliday?'

'Yes. It was a kind of holiday,' she said, looking up.

'I need also. No chance.'

He left her alone then. Sometimes he was more talkative. He had his disgruntled face on. She didn't know his name, or he hers, but she knew his expressions.

Her phone was switched to silent. Fran had been frantically texting her, dying to know about the wedding. Anita had agreed to meet up for a drink the following week. She could always cancel. Laurence had also been in contact with her. She wasn't quite ready for Laurence. She told him she was a bit low and would get in touch when she was better.

She took time over drinking the coffee. The banquette was like a berth and the room like a cabin. After a spell away, routine was simple. Each hour known; fresh and stale overlapped. Her GP had agreed to prescribe a limited amount of diazepam and something to take in a panic attack. Anita had form for mental illness. Dr Ali had glanced at her hair and frowned. On the whole, she felt calmer.

'How was Bulgaria?' Joe Brabazon-Morley, the gallery owner, stood, swaying in the doorway to his office, one hand high on the frame, the other on his hip. He anchored himself, as if on a boat in bad weather. Aspects of the interior behind him came and went, shelved catalogues, stacked paintings, box files. It was a sliver of a room with no natural light; crammed and shipshape.

'Interesting,' Anita said.

'You were travelling around, weren't you? Where were you based?'

'By the Black Sea. A kind of fishing village turned resort.'

'Very *fin de saison*, I imagine.'

'Yes, totally.'

Anita thought of the seaside bars, not just locked but boxed up for the winter months, and the concrete jetty that stretched out into the sea.

'We went to Sofia once. We were bowled over by the menus. "Mince pie" was top of the main courses. We thought Christmas had come early – but it turned out to be some kind of moussaka. My wife and I used to play a little guessing game.' Joe lurched forward. '"Small, flat, slightly singed loaf"? That was another one.'

'Toast I should think,' Anita said.

'Gosh. I see you went native. We never got as good as that.'

'No, I've been home to Hampshire. That's how the toast is there.'

Joe guffawed.

Anita had imagined Joe's wife as a sturdy person who could steady his perpetual movement or, in extremis, prop him up – but she had been wrong. Ruth had turned up at the gallery one morning. She was a serene, girl-sized woman, who wore Shaker-style clothes and kept her own space, like a dancer. She never came to the gallery previews. Joe said she wasn't a party girl.

'Before I retreat to my scullery, Anita: the February exhibition. Aylmer Dunn's family. They are playing silly buggers with the studio estate paintings. I may have to go to Devon. So it's "A Good Thing" you're back. Nathan is a sweetie but too young to be left "In Charge".'

'Where is Nathan?' Anita asked.

'He has a cold,' Joe said. 'Sneezing all over the place, yesterday.'

'Oh.'

So he was still *in situ*, the serious twenty-one-year-old

243

who had done her job for the last month. As an intern, wholly subsidised by his parents, he cost Joe the price of a daily sandwich. Joe hadn't told Anita she was no longer wanted but it was probably only a matter of time. There were plenty of Nathans available. Anita sometimes thought of going out east – East London, that is, Hoxton or Shoreditch – where the freshest art was sold. But they were young over there; young and energetic. She would be out of her depth, knowing only modern British.

The gallery was showing works by Bernard Wellman RA. Anita had missed the party though she had been involved in the preparations for the exhibition. A handful of paintings had been sold – doors opening on to gardens. They always went first – offering a way out.

Joe was back in his room and talking on the telephone. Anita could hear him shuffling through papers as he conversed. Whole mornings went by without clients. The gallery was generally quiet until late afternoon – especially at the beginning of the week. Shepherd Market lacked the passing trade of Mayfair proper; the convoys of taxis. Sometimes one of Joe's chums turned up, then Joe would spring out from his room at the back, flick back his hair and conduct a tour, mixing it with gossip. He was never less than entranced by the art.

Anita studied the catalogue. Bernard Wellman's paintings looked more at home on the page than hanging on the wall, she thought. They had an illustrative quality that suited a book format. The images turned into recognisable people and places too soon – and then where to look? A batsman at the wicket – the same batsman locked in thought outside a pavilion – the harbour wall at Walberswick – Chapman's Pool, Dorset – the Thames at Chiswick.

Wellman's cricketer was handsome in an interwar years kind of way. The high forehead, the vulnerable neck, slicked with blue shadow. His Adam's apple was exposed like a flesh wound. Anita began to add him to the landscapes. He crept in, while remaining outside the frame. She linked up the sequence into a kind of narrative. The cricketer was a presence for a time, then a loss.

She saw Bernard Wellman RA in a new light – and turned to the biog on the back inside cover:

1929 Elected Associate of the Watercolour Society.

1932 Married Dora Brown, former sculpture student at the RCA.

1937 Appointed Honorary Secretary of the New English Art Club.

1950 Elected Associate of the Royal Academy.

The elections and appointments continued – and the births of several sons – travel in the southern hemisphere – a second marriage, twin daughters. Little time for cricketers – or even painting. Anita amended her story to, 'Knocked off another quick *Door Into Garden.*'

There was something outrageous about potted biography. As if life proceeded in a line. Anita saw time more as loops and circles with the centre of the circles somewhat elusive. They were stones thrown into a pool; the ripples intersected. She saw her own life in that way and was prepared to extend it to the lives of others, though the thinking became quite complicated. At least from the outside, many people seemed to go by the forward-step model, crossing off the To Do list. It struck her as strangely old-fashioned, like belonging to the Flat Earth Society.

11

Anita returned to Hampshire for Christmas. Granny Randall was brought out for the day. She asked where her father was and when Veronica said he was dead, gave a little twitch. She smiled bravely, as though she had known all along. She needed to be shepherded – from the high-seated armchair in the drawing room, to the dining room, to the lavatory – several times, which gave structure to the proceedings. Barney and Kendra had gone to the States.

Emma had her baby on the 8th of January. He was a boy, Bevis, who weighed four point two kilos. The announcement came on a card, printed with a photo of newborn Bevis tucked in the crook of a smooth arm; Emma's presumably.

In the same post, Anita received an envelope addressed in unfamiliar handwriting. It turned out to be from Laurence; a printed prayer from the Coptic liturgy of St Cyril with the initial letter in the style of an illuminated manuscript. Scrawled across the bottom he had written, *Anita, Hope you feel better soon, Laurence*. Anita was astonished. She felt terrible that she had sent him bogus photographs and that he had sent her a prayer. She wrote back by text to say thank you and tried to forget about it.

She went shopping in King's Road, Chelsea, one evening after work. The sales were on and the street was crowded. People were encumbered by sharp-cornered bags that they used as light weaponry. The twinkly Christmas lights in the plane trees had vanished; put away for another year. Anita fought her way along the pavement and into shops that sold baby clothes. She avoided the racks of marked-down goods and sought out the non-sale stock, generally at the back of a shop, where the few mint-condition garments clung to respectability at decent spaces from each other. Anita fingered the miniature clothes. She pulled them from the rail and held them up, unable to decide on size or colour, and finally came away with a brown cashmere jumper for a three-to-six-month-old. It was more expensive than it looked and required hand washing. Later, she wrapped it in tissue paper and posted it to Wandsworth. Emma would have enough visitors. Anita didn't want to barge in.

Towards the end of the month, Nick and Emma invited Anita to a late breakfast at the café by Wandsworth Common where they had met in October.

They were indoors this time and the place was full of buggies. James and Stella were there with their son, also another couple, Lydia and Christian, with their baby, Gerald.

Bevis was out of sight, buried under a mound of duvet, with the pram hood up. Anita admired him.

'We should have asked you round to ours,' Emma whispered when Anita bent to kiss her, 'but it's really nice to get out of the house.'

Anita unwound her scarf and took off her coat. Another chair was added. Anita wedged herself in.

'He'll wake up soon,' Emma said. 'He never goes for longer than three hours.'

'You can get a lot done in three hours. Make the most of it,' Stella said. 'Frankie, don't do that. It's disgusting. James, can you stop Frankie spitting on the table.'

'Not really,' James said.

Frankie's eyes rolled round and looked at his father. The gob that had emerged from his mouth dried on his chin.

Nick handed Anita a menu. 'Have you met Lydia and Christian?'

He gestured in a genial way and Lydia – a snub-nosed woman with a curtain of red hair – said hello to Anita, as if she had won a definitive game of stones, scissors and paper, and resumed her conversation with James.

Christian, with Gerald on his knee, was content to exchange basic information.

'What should I be buying?' he asked when he heard Anita worked in an art gallery.

People often asked that and she loyally stuck up for modern British.

'They're dead, all your artists?' Christian asked.

Anita agreed that most of them were. She told him that Joe had once shown the work of a Royal Academician who was in a care home in Hindhead and had reached his hundredth birthday. He had come to the preview with his daughter and kept asking when the boat was sailing. 'Take me below. You did book a stateroom didn't you, Eliza? I'm not sitting up all the way to Trinidad.'

Christian laughed. 'That will be me one day. I'm already doing that thing, going into a room and forgetting what I went for.'

'My granny used to say, "Shoot me if I go demented," but we haven't – obviously,' Anita said.

'You've still got her by the sound of things. A long-lived family,' Christian said.

'Mostly,' Anita said.

'Weren't you going off somewhere when we last saw you?' Stella addressed Anita.

'Bulgaria,' Anita said.

'Oh yes, Bansko,' James said.

'How was it?' Stella asked.

'It was all right,' Anita said. 'As you might imagine, really.'

She was aware that this was inadequate. The others waited for more – because it was impossible that anyone should have so little to say.

'Anita was taking photos of clapped-out buildings. She drove to remote places and trespassed on people's land,' Nick said.

He was sitting on the opposite side of the table from Anita. His face was bland, quite ordinary. He had always had less particular looks than her brothers. But between one glance and the next, his features sharpened into beauty. She never understood how that happened; it was like a trick of the light.

'How brave,' Stella said. 'I hate driving anywhere I don't know. Aren't the signs in a different alphabet? My idea of a nightmare.'

'Nicholas told me this incredible story about some woodcutter turning up while Anita was inside his house,' Emma said. 'He wasn't wearing any trousers.'

'Good Lord.' Christian, whose son was now using him as a climbing wall, looked at Anita with interest. Gerald had reached his father's glasses and was wresting them from his nose.

'It didn't really happen like that,' Anita said.

'She was very calm,' Emma said.

'As long as you don't break into a house, it's not a criminal offence. That's why squatters don't get arrested. Having said that, it might not be the same in Bulgaria,' Stella said.

'You can probably bribe the judge,' James said.

'It's outrageous, when you think about it, that people can just move into your property.' Lydia swept her hair from her face before continuing. 'I dread that happening to us. We're doing a major renovation this spring and won't have a back to the house.'

'Squatters can't access the utilities.' Christian spoke from between Gerald's fat, corduroy-covered legs. 'As soon as they do, the police can charge them.'

'I don't suppose Anita ran a bath,' Nick said.

Everyone was being kind. It was a shame that she didn't deserve the kindness. She had come home from Bulgaria early, having ballsed up the driving, and taken fraudulent photographs in outer London suburbs. Although the trip had been flight – sheer escapism – she had hoped to make a success of it. She wished she were the intrepid woman they thought she was.

'So whatever did you say when this woodcutter person turned up? You were in a really vulnerable position,' Stella said.

'Oh, I just got in the car and left. It wasn't at all dramatic,' Anita said.

'She has a reckless streak.' Nick smiled at her.

Anita had some notion that after a long enough gap, her relationship with Nick would stop shooting out random signals. How long, she had no idea; she had never run like a well-oiled machine. Whatever there was between them had no name; Mark's one-time friend; her teenage idol. They had been lovers between April and July. These were elements of a relationship that could only be defined by a longish explanatory sentence. Friends' friends could become your friends but siblings' friends came with an asterisk next to their names. When you checked the reference it was too complex to follow; bedevilled by subclauses, like a piece of legislation.

12

'Mossy, what are you doing on your own?' Izzy grabbed her arm. 'Nicholas, stop being useful and come and talk to Mossy.'

Anita turned. A man was standing by a long trestle table. The white cloth that covered it was anchored with clips. The man twisted a cork from a bottle of Prosecco. They were at a lunch party in a garden in Sussex.

'Give Mossy a refill, then I'll take the bottle,' Izzy said. 'I can't believe this weather. In April. We're so lucky. When we planned this I thought we'd all be stuck inside by the fire.'

The cork came out with a pop and Nicholas caught the foamy liquid in one of the empty glasses. His shirt-sleeves were rolled up. He had nice arms.

Nicholas turned and came towards Izzy and Anita. As he poured, angling the bottle, Anita recognised him.

'We have met,' she said.

'Brilliant,' Izzy said, bearing the bottle away to other guests.

'Remind me,' he said.

He still had the knack of instant but lazy engagement. There was a latching. But Anita had known, at the age of thirteen, that it wasn't specific to her.

'Anita Mostyn?' She rolled the stem of the glass between her fingers.

He took a gulp of wine.

'You came to stay – about, oh, I don't know, twenty-something years ago,' she said. 'You were friends with my brother. Mark Mostyn.'

'The little sister. Anita. Of course. I know exactly who you are.' He was suddenly smiling. Then his face fell. She knew what was coming. 'I'm sorry. About Mark.'

She nodded and stared straight at his shirt buttons. 'Izzy's new house is lovely, isn't it?' she said when she raised her eyes.

'Look, Anita, it's incredible to see you. Let's talk. I'd love to talk to you. We'll move out of the line of fire.'

He took her hand and steered her away from the house and down the first set of steps.

The garden was wide and followed the descending slope of the land. Three long terraces – rectangular lawned areas divided by low brick walls – had been cut into the hillside. The lowest level of the garden was rough grass and a small orchard of old fruit trees; beyond the boundary were fields and an uninterrupted view of the South Downs.

'Are you on your own? I mean, do you have someone with you?' he asked.

'No,' she said.

'Neither do I. My girlfriend's got food poisoning. You are so recognisable as the same person, Anita. It's incredible.'

The unoccupied rugs scattered over the lawn looked provisional, like magic carpets that were waiting to take off. He led her past them and round the guests who stood, drinking. They walked until they reached the last low brick wall; the limit of the cultivated part of the garden. On the other side was an overgrown asparagus bed. Gnarled old fruit trees rose from long grass. Their leaves were just showing. He let go of her hand.

'I lost touch with Mark. I wish I'd kept up. I liked him,' Nick said.

'He was furious that time you went to a New Year's Eve party with Barney. Do you remember?'

'Barney. I'd forgotten that name. How is he? What's he up to?'

'Divorced. Making money . . .'

'No. Tell me about him later. Let's go back to the beginning. Tell me about Mark.'

*

They talked for over an hour. She talked mostly. Nick listened. The words didn't come out as a story – at least not to her. The experience of Barney's first wedding was still with her; formless, yet vital. She was maimed by reliving it and, afterwards – in an aura of doubleness – barely remembered anything she had said.

Anita sometimes referred to Mark's accident with people who knew – though mostly not. With strangers she was reticent. If the brothers and sisters question cropped up, she spoke of Barney. Why kill a conversation? On the occasions when she had said something, she regretted it. Her interlocutors were embarrassed, or probing, or offered some quite dissimilar experience in exchange. There were a hundred ways to get it wrong. She didn't blame them. Then, out of nowhere – nine years later – Nick Halsey.

If you meet someone again after a long, long gap, you have to join up two impressions of that person and also two separate versions of self. Merging the young Nick Halsey with the man her friend Izzy had introduced Anita to had been like watching a photograph develop in a bath of chemicals.

'Come on, you two. Come and grab some pudding,' Izzy called.

Anita and Nick were still in the same spot in the old orchard. Nick had gone over to collect food for them both and they had eaten, sitting in long grass.

Anita scanned the scene in front of her, as if waking from a dream – or falling back into one. She squinted at the sun, as if she rarely got out in fine weather. The garden came into focus: groups of people, arranged in patterns on the rugs. She saw them as characters in a silent film. They appeared to be talking and digging into dessert. After a delay, her hearing caught up. She recognised the sound of voices in open air and the chink of spoons on bowls. Children raced around, whooping. They dodged grown-ups and ice buckets. They leapt over rugs. It was a good place for chasing though not for football. The brick house was the backdrop – long and low with Arts and Crafts-style gables and square casement windows.

'Right. Let's go,' Nick said.

They got up and climbed over the low wall. Side by side, they went up the steps in the terraces and walked over to the long trestle table – to find that lunch had ended. The white tablecloth was spattered with food and crumbs, the platters of air-freighted berries half empty, lemon tarts reduced to misshapen slices. One or two people were helping themselves to seconds. A little boy scooped up ice cream that had turned into a diminishing island in a milky lake.

Izzy, trying to bring some order to the table, was putting the remaining slices of tart on to one platter. She gave Anita a look. A visible gulp and a widening of the eyes, as if to say 'Where have you been?' or 'Whoa.' Conveying something.

Anita put some unseasonal raspberries in a bowl. She felt different, as if her limbs were disordered, or parts of her missing.

She went to join Piers, Izzy's husband, who was sitting in a small group. A man with a shock of pale blond hair was holding forth. He wore red spectacles. Nick set off in a different direction. Piers introduced her briefly and the man continued. Anita tried to concentrate. The voice was insistent like an ultra-bright colour. Stone Age man must have spent a lot of time pontificating. It was a successful strategy; more potent, in its way, than sexual attraction. People gathered round and that was the beginning of society. No one asked Anita's opinion. She sat there with her bare legs tucked under her, holding her pudding bowl.

A child ran across the lawn, as if tigers were after him.

'There goes Waldo,' someone said.

Piers got up from the grass and went off to make coffee.

A man, sitting cross-legged nearby, spoke to Anita. 'So how do you know Izzy and Piers?' he asked, sotto voce, so as not to disturb the blond orator.

She told him. They carried on a conversation. He spoke. She spoke. Once or twice they both laughed. The spectacles glinted in the sun.

After the coffee had been drunk, there was a loosening in the party. The guests began to shift. Having stood up, some of them realised that there were friends present they hadn't talked to. This caused a resurgence of hellos and catching up, almost as though the party were beginning all over again. Children who had boldly made friends with each other and vanished into remote parts of the garden had to be found. Others, napping on rugs, were roused from sleep.

Anita looked around for Nick. She couldn't leave without saying goodbye to him. He was standing by the door to the kitchen, in conversation with a woman who wore a floppy white sun hat. She was chopping the air with her hand as she spoke.

Anita approached.

'I simply don't accept that two As and a B from a comprehensive are worth the same, or more, than three A stars from Winchester,' the woman was saying. 'And they say there's no dumbing down!'

'Excuse me, I must just talk to Anita.' Nick turned towards her. 'You're not going, are you? Now? How are you getting back?' he said.

'By train.'

'I'll give you a lift to the station,' Nick said.

The woman looked right through Anita. Her eyes under the hat were fixed and unseeing, as though a beautician were applying mascara to them. Anita didn't mind. A goodbye carried out in a cloud of disapproval protected her. She had no expectations of Nick Halsey – and nothing to add. She was resolute against any kind of postscript. She had no wish to 'take care' of herself or exchange jokey variants on 'Let's not leave it another twenty years.'

'No, I'll be fine. The station's not far,' Anita said. 'Thank you for offering.'

'Or drive you to London. Look, don't go by train. It's absurd,' Nick said.

The woman twisted her head away with a pained expression on her face.

Anita had, all those years ago, picked right. His not being the kind of person who would let her go in disarray was why she had been able to talk to him about Mark. Her thirteen-year-old skewness had identified him. Which set her wondering what might have happened had he and Mark remained friends and whether Nick might not have had some Gaston/Gigi, 'Zank Heaven for Leetle Girls' moment that would have landed them together in a state of perpetual bliss and ongoing communication. Absurd, of course. That was a rewrite of gross sentimentality. It could never have happened and – stretching incredulity – had it happened, they would have come adrift, as couples do, and then losing the person she could talk to freely – the atrophy of the magical thread – would have sunk her.

She recalled the group therapy sessions when she had the breakdown after Mark's death. All those bungled stories that were stuttered out; she had done her best to add to them. She had started from the wrong end, somehow; not having known the right entry point to come in. A well-meaning 'Don't blame yourself', she dreaded. She needed to be blamed. But she wasn't eloquent. Words dripped unreliably, like water through a blocked gutter. She longed for a downpour. The facilitator prompted and nine times out of ten, she thought, for God's sake, why mention *that*? – and lost the drift.

She had trouble conveying Veronica. They, many of them, had issues with their mothers. If it wasn't their mums, it was their dads and often the whole cringe-making set-up. They all thought Veronica was the pits, though Anita hadn't set out to show her in a bad light. Her mother's dignity in the aftermath of Mark's accident came across icily. Veronica had refused to hear her apologies.

'He had had too much to drink, Anita. It's as simple as that. The rest was an accident. You had no part in it – are you listening to me? Absolutely no part.'

The group thought that was cold. 'But she didn't listen to *you*,' they said.

'Maybe not. But she forgave me,' Anita said, 'which is more important, isn't it? She couldn't stand the howling.'

She tried to explain that Veronica had become a bit more like Granny; older and kinder. She remembered to hug her daughter occasionally, though the hugs weren't too convincing – and, on the whole, she had stopped commenting on Anita's appearance and stupidity.

'Well, if that's an improvement,' one of them said, 'she must have been total crap before.'

Jim, the facilitator, had done his best, though Anita found it distracting that he had trouble with his contact lenses and would abruptly turn to one side, as if about to vomit over the side of the chair. Then his hand would go up to his eye. He grimaced, pulled his bottom eyelid and let the tiny lens fall invisibly into his hand. Sometimes he blinked and reinserted it but mostly he sat for the rest of the session with the lens perched on his open palm. Anita knew he couldn't be listening with one half of his sight displaced. She wouldn't have been able to listen. It was hard enough dealing with one's own ongoing thoughts without seeing through an eye darkly; the glass elsewhere. Not being able to identify the contact lens was also disturbing. Unless you were next to Jim in the circle, it remained imperceptible; dead to the light of the overhead fluorescent tubes. As a phantom object, it became the focus of the session. Was it there, or wasn't it? Anita considered the possibility that the balancing act was a pretence and that Jim's professionalism restrained him from scrabbling around on the floor. She found herself scanning the grey vinyl and the dustballs that gathered under the chairs.

The woman in the hat had gone. It was just the two of them.

'Let's go then, Anita,' Nick said. 'Izzy's just over there. I think I saw Piers go into the kitchen. We'll say goodbye and leave.'

For the second time that afternoon, he took Anita's hand and led her away.

13

'Do you drive, Anita?' Nick made it sound quite natural if she didn't.

They were on a lane, stuck behind a lorry and had just passed signs to Uckfield. A convoy of vehicles trailed behind them. Trees lined the route; their branches met. In the summer, full-sized leaves would overlap and keep out the sun.

'Yes, but I've never liked driving,' Anita said. 'It's something I make myself do. I went on holiday to Ireland last year – the Galway peninsula – and the person I was with did something to his ankle so I ended up the sole driver.'

'A man, then, not just a person?' Nick was changing up and down between low gears as the cars ahead lurched between moving and braking.

'Did I say person? How disingenuous. Anyway, the driving wasn't what went wrong with the holiday.'

Nick's car made expensive noises. Its engine intoned a low note. There were subtle electronic clickings. The air con hummed. Windows were shut to keep the cold in. Anita hadn't noticed the exterior or the make but inside was clean and new, as if recently valeted. She had longed to go in the old car Nick Halsey brought to Kingsfold. She had envied Mark and Barney. Now, none of that mattered.

She didn't know what Nick's job was, or where he lived, or how he knew Izzy and Piers. He was also short of similar information about her, though he would find out her address by taking her to the house in Chelsea. Perhaps he would drop her off at some convenient spot in London that would save him going out of his way. She would suggest this later. The weighting of what each of them knew about the other was unbalanced. He had known her parents and brothers. He had stayed in their house. What else? She had talked all afternoon.

She was drained now – and wondered what he would do with her outpouring, and where it would go. Her memories – the words and pictures that bounced around in her head, floating, tumbling and covered in sticky bits that adhered to her life – she had handed over to him. They needed validation. In Nick's mind, they would live a calmer existence; kept in an orderly storehouse and retrieved, if at all, like facts. She wanted him to make everything all right.

She had once observed him closely. Between the ages of thirteen and fifteen, she had known a lot about him. His eyes, his skin, the way he moved.

He had a girlfriend with food poisoning.

'Was it the first time you'd been away together?' Nick seemed amused. 'You and this fellow.'

'Yes, it was, as it happens,' Anita said.

'Good to find out sooner rather than later that you didn't get on.'

'How do you know we hadn't been seeing each other for years?'

'You gave a few clues,' Nick said.

She didn't mind talking about Matt Woodall, who, since the holiday, had turned into a comedy act. Fran had seen the episode as another example of Mossy being a bad picker. Her Tim was so normal. Well, Fran thought so.

'He got annoyed that I was so hopeless at overtaking,' Anita said.

'They drive in the middle of the road there.'

'Yes, they do. It's not just a myth. But I am bad at overtaking. We went along in a kind of funeral cortège of pent-up boredom, behind some old guy in a hat. Only, Matt was bored and seething, and I was bored and nervous.'

'Sounds like hell.'

'It was actually. He sat there resenting. Until – don't worry, I'm not going to do what he did – he suddenly shouted, "Fuck this. Just do it, Anita," and whacked the dashboard. Needless to say, I drove clean off the road.'

'Hit anything?'

'Luckily not. But one wheel was in the ditch. The car was totally lopsided. We both got out. That was the moment to laugh, or make up. But we didn't. The sun had come out. There was cow parsley everywhere and may blossom. Paradise, in a way.'

'In a way,' Nick echoed and laughed.

They were moving again. Traffic ahead had unstuck. Nick shifted slightly and stretched his legs. Anita remembered that they would get to London, in maybe less than an hour.

The pause in conversation carried on and the silence between them was restful. She was relieved he hadn't returned to the subject of Mark, though when Izzy called time on them she had stopped, as if suddenly at the edge of a high sea cliff. She felt cheated of an ending. But, as long as consciousness lasted, there were no endings, only interruptions.

She hadn't reached Mark's death; had barely touched on all those months of going to Rayley Park Clinic. Time had meant nothing and everything in that place. Visitors planned to stay for a couple of hours, or return the following Tuesday. They counted the weeks. They kept vigil.

Mark hadn't quite made twelve months. The infection that turned to pneumonia took little from him, only his breath.

The Mostyns had never gone back there. The Friends of Rayley Park Clinic was one committee that Veronica had no wish to be on. It was thriving, according to newsletters that turned up at her parents' house. Fund-raising fetes, a summer tea party, a Christmas-carol evening with mince pies and mulled wine. These events were recorded.

When he turned off the road Anita said nothing. The land rose and fell in shallow folds, cut with chalk. They put the visors down because they were facing westward and the sun caught the windscreen. Where the contours allowed, vistas of low hills appeared in the distance. The breeze had blown the air clean as a glass. The hills lay like bands of shadow stretched just below the horizon, hiding London.

The track, level to begin with, became uneven; a background of dips and crunches that jolted them around the car. Nick changed up and down between low gears and swore in a perfunctory way when the car lurched badly.

'Ashdown Forest,' he said. 'Ever been here?'

'No. There aren't many trees, for a forest,' she said. 'Oh, maybe there are some up ahead.'

She sat on her hands, staring out at the heathland;

a choppy sea of gorse and bracken in tufty hummocks. The copse came closer – not smoothly but in fits and starts because of their shook-up means of travelling.

As they entered the woodland, passing between the first trees, Nick turned off the air con and pressed the control that lowered the windows. Damp warmth washed into the car and the air felt like spring again. They came across a dip in the track; a jagged-edged hollow where the sandy soil had caved in. Nick steered round it, crushing the bracken, and began to whistle between his teeth.

He stopped the car, sliding it to a halt on spongy soil. Anita looked down at herself, as if at someone else's body. The bare legs, the flimsy skirt, creased by sitting on grass.

She saw his hand move towards her. It crept from her hip to her waist, to her breast. It was splayed across her back when he leant across and kissed her.

They both got out quickly, leaving the doors open. Heat came off the car, as from a huge free-standing radiator that continued to shudder as it cooled. The inland clearing, miles from the sea and from London, might have been in the middle of a continent.

The car tyres, next to them, heated from the journey, gave off a smell of hot rubber. She was in Nick's shadow. A shaft of daylight, straight as a thread, dropped through the branches on to him. She had no idea who she was, a girl, or a woman; no one. In her mind, she was nothing. Then they were on the ground, his feet on hers, his body poised over her.

14

Frankie was snapping coloured crayons the waiter had provided. The spitting had stopped. New people had piled in to the café and were grouped around the door, in their outdoor clothes, waiting for tables. Behind the counter, the coffee frother worked full pelt. Down the length of the room, adults kept conversations going, in spite of their children. They talked from odd positions, leaning sideways, half under the table, jiggling up and down. They maintained flow, loudly, without hesitation or interruption, as though they were on live radio. A waiter stretched up to the blackboard on the wall and rubbed out the chalked words *Sausage Baguette*.

At Anita's table, the coffee had arrived, together with plates of croissants and pains au chocolat. James waited for poached eggs. The focus had shifted away from Anita. They were talking among themselves now – which suited her. Discussion based on her recent foreign experiences had died out like a fuelless fire. She had offered no impressions or anecdotes.

She had never told Nick Halsey that he had once

consumed her. There would perhaps have been a way of saying it lightly. He might have been flattered – and amused. But the thought of making the topic flattering and amusing repelled her. She hadn't wanted to burden him – or herself – with what seemed like too much information. No one wanted to know that they fed a fantasy life, did they? 'I wasted hours thinking about you' was not a sentence much said.

Instead, she had matched Nick's breeziness. They were harmless to each other; effortfully harmless. She had sensed his alarm. When he turned the car radio on – *Poetry Please* – she had looked up and seen his eyes. A verse-reading voice blared out through the speakers. Anita was still trembling. Nick turned down the volume. The sound was diminished but not the self-conscious, chummy delivery, which persisted, full of intent. As a post-coital calmative it was a failure but it somehow got them back on to the A22.

So the gesture towards the on/off radio button both was and wasn't a dismissal or a matter-of-fact cutting of mood. Anita saw it both ways. Their subsequent brief affair was, from the start, a taming. Nick Halsey was a family man, not a dangerous one – and during the weeks when they met for sex, had found the time to engender Bevis.

He had wanted to stay in touch, which was why she was with him and Emma now in the café that overlooked Wandsworth Common. She saw a point to it. The

273

connection with the past. She thought about lost years; not the undocumented time of famous types like Jesus or Shakespeare, but the stretches that people go through, pulled out of true, because something has gone so wrong that they just mark time, waiting for pain to go away.

She didn't feel she was special – or relish some secret special connection with Nick. Her upbringing made her proof against that. She would never overinterpret a look. To Emma she remained the sister of Nick's old friend who had died: Mark Mostyn. Since the chance meeting at Izzy and Piers's house-warming, Anita had been included in their circle.

'Any more travel plans?' Christian asked her.

Gerald had come to rest again and was sucking a teaspoon. His round eyes focused upwards, as on a beatific vision.

'No. I'll stay put now,' Anita replied.

'Good thinking. Our travelling is curtailed by this one, but we've got skiing in February and Syria to look forward to at Easter. Gerald's fairly intrepid, aren't you, boy? We'd really like to buy somewhere; maybe in France or Italy. One day.' Christian spread apricot jam on his croissant.

'Something's often wrong in a rented property. No bedside lamps. Or weird bathroom arrangements,' Anita said.

'Exactly. Lydia's parents have a place in the Limousin

so we can sneak a free one – but, of course, they're there. Jane and Alan.'

'My mother's a morning person and talks for England,' Emma said. 'I feel so sorry for Nicholas. He's very sweet to her.'

'Outhouses are the way forward,' Stella said. 'James, watch Frankie with that pain au chocolat.'

'Really? Is that where you stick your in-laws?' Christian asked.

'No, of course not, Christian,' Stella said. 'But we have friends with a villa in Tuscany, and they've converted their outhouses into lovely self-contained wings so that guests can do their own thing.'

'Marvellous,' Christian said.

'It's my dream to have spare unused space for a project,' Emma said.

'I'd segregate the nanny,' Lydia said.

'Think ahead,' Christian said. 'They do grow up, you know. How about a den for teenagers and their emergent rock bands?'

'Will you be in a rock band, Frankie?' Nick asked the little boy.

'No,' Frankie said, stabbing his fingers into chocolate. 'No, no, no.'

'You'd like a few barns to muck about in, wouldn't you?' Christian asked.

'Burn 'em wiv a match!' Frankie shouted.

'I'm afraid he is into fire at the moment,' Stella said.

'It's water with my nephews,' Christian said. 'I can't tell you how many times they've flooded the basement. My sister has cascades through the light fittings, like special effects. Her husband thinks she's having an affair with the loss adjuster. The man practically lives there.'

Frankie drummed his feet against the chair legs and worked his arms, as though conducting a hellish passage in a symphony.

15

In a Clerkenwell wine bar, Anita showed Laurence Beament photos of Bevis.

'Whose infant are we looking at?' Laurence glanced at her phone.

'Nick and Emma's. Emma sent them. He's wearing the jumper I gave him. He's ten weeks and it already fits him. Isn't he ginormous?'

She prattled on. Laurence, in a dark suit and a primrose yellow tie dotted with cats and dogs, had come straight from work. *Meet up at 17.45*, he had written, which was why the long communal tables made of reclaimed wood were empty. Outside, a few smokers clustered, drinking under the awning, sheltering from rain. Anita had arrived early, preferring to be the one *in situ*. Laurence had turned up on time, kissed Anita's cheek and gone to the bar for drinks. Returning, he had swung his legs awkwardly over the bench to sit down beside her. The clean expanse of table stretched away, like a lab bench. In front of them were two almost empty glasses of wine and the evening newspaper that Anita had picked up at Farringdon Station.

Laurence had made several attempts to see her. She couldn't put a meeting off for ever, so when he suggested a drink, rather than dinner, she had agreed. She had been feeling slightly calmer lately and was off the diazepam.

Bevis failed to interest Laurence. Anita put her phone away and changed the subject. She told him about Nathan. 'He looks about twelve years old. Quite pompous. He can't believe we don't have an important client list. He wants to know who's on it. Joe smiles enigmatically and says he's old school. All his clients are equal.'

'That's bollocks isn't it? Who is on it?'

'No one famous.'

Laurence nodded. His mind was elsewhere. Anita felt uneasy. Laurence looked thinner. He had acquired a well-defined waist. She thought of the photographs and the prayer of St Cyril – not the words but the fact that Laurence had sent it – and wondered if he had become religious and was fasting for Lent. He hadn't given up drinking. He was knocking the wine back. She wished he weren't sitting so close. She shifted to make space between them. He continued to face forward, like a boy at a school desk, and occasionally swivelled his head to look at her. Sideways on, his gooseberry eyes seemed to bulge more.

'Tell me about Dobrich,' he said. 'Did you enjoy it?'

He sounded deeply bored, as though asking the question out of duty.

'Your apartment is gorgeous, Larry. Really lovely. A private terrace, everything brand new. I felt really spoiled,' she twittered.

'And the driving? The car turned up all right?'

'Yes. It all worked perfectly.'

'Good.'

'I'm not the world's best driver. But I managed. I avoided the worst of the potholes.'

'Potholes. People always seem to mention them.' He stroked the tie. 'They've become a kind of cliché.'

'I expect someone will get round to mending them.' She laughed gaily. 'There seemed to be all kinds of EU initiatives. They'll be a thing of the past. Like London fog.'

'Where did you eat?' he asked in the same brassed-off tone of voice.

'Everywhere seemed to be shut. I bought stuff from a little shop down near the harbour and cooked in your beautiful kitchen. I suppose I could have investigated somewhere further down the coast but after driving all day . . .' She tailed off.

'The Captain Cook stays open all year. I should have mentioned that. The food's mediocre but the place has its charms.' Laurence paused. 'Not that it would have helped. Seeing you weren't there. You never went, did you?'

She was astounded. 'But of course I was there, Larry. Whatever do you mean?'

'Let me get you another drink, Mossy.' He began to extricate himself from the bench.

'No, it's my turn. Stay there.' Shocked though she was, she couldn't stand a repeat of the leg-swinging business. 'What was it?'

'What was what?'

'The wine.'

'House red. It's perfectly drinkable here. Argentinian.'

She walked towards the bar in a trance and wondered whether to bolt. The doors were open, the al fresco drinkers – by now more numerous – grouped on the pavement. Competitive voice-raising, male dominated, rose under the awning; a siren call. She longed to be out there, crushed between suits and screened by smoke. The street beyond, fresh with drizzle, led to Clerkenwell Road. Buses and taxis swished past in a tantalising blur of moving lights.

There were probably penalties for putting false information on a website. Had Laurence already been charged? She would pay the fine, and take full responsibility. She would have a criminal record but that wouldn't matter. She could put up with anything but the present moment.

At the bar, Anita allowed three people to push in front of her. She stood there, dazed. In her mind, she scrolled through the pictures. The one-off properties she had discovered in Hertfordshire. She remembered the farm buildings and how pleased she had been to come across the white goat.

The barman turned to serve her. His head was shaved; all but a triangular-shaped piece that hung over one eye. He smirked as if he knew about the goat; as if it had materialised and was roaming about in the background, rubbing against the benches. With a dry mouth, Anita ordered. She reminded herself that though emotions were revealed in the face, individual items, however vivid, stayed hidden. No doubt, the barman had a fantasy life of his own, though it wouldn't involve rural Dobrich.

He bent under the counter and produced an open bottle. She fumbled in her bag and found a twenty-pound note. Her hands shook as she passed the money to him and when the moment came to pick up the glasses, she steeled herself into steadiness, not wanting to spill or slop wine, like someone with delirium tremens.

Through the sound of raised voices, she heard the tap of her heels. The walk across the smooth wooden floor seemed long but, as she reached the table, not long enough. She put the two glasses down, attempted a smile

281

and sat down opposite Laurence. This was a type of interview. It was best to look him straight in the eye.

After a sip, Laurence took to glass gazing. Anita's instinct was to begin the apologies but she checked herself. The seconds turned into minutes.

'Tell me about St Cyril,' she said, cautiously.

'Oh, did you like that? The card's been knocking about on my mantelpiece. It was a memento from the white church with the bell tower – which you didn't see,' he added pointedly.

'Who was he?' she asked.

Laurence embarked on a disquisition that began with Khan Boris's rapprochement with Byzantium. He assumed a headmasterly, more-in-sorrow-than-in-anger expression, but his voice sounded normal. He established a flow.

Anita was sorry, in a way, that the prayer was just something from his mantelpiece. Part of her wanted certainty; stern reproach followed by absolution. Mostly, she wanted to get clean away. She stopped herself from looking at the door and tried to breathe steadily. She wondered how long she could depend on the saving power of facts as a diversion tactic.

'Must have been tough for Methodius that the alphabet ended up being called "Cyrillic" not "Methodical",' she said, brightly.

'I believe it only happened once both the brothers were

dead,' Laurence replied. 'Methodius wouldn't have known.'

'I imagine that if you are related to a saint the information somehow gets through,' Anita said.

Laurence smoothed the back of his neck. 'I came to The Hesperia, Mossy,' he said.

'When?' she asked quickly.

'During your so-called stay. The seventeenth of November to be precise.' His intonation had turned flat and expressionless again.

She took a breath. 'I was probably out. You should have said you were coming. It was a bit random, just turning up, Larry.'

'The apartment was untouched. I knew straight away you hadn't been there,' he said.

'But I was there.'

'Oh, Mossy . . .'

'You let yourself in?' she asked.

'Yes, why not?'

'Is that all?'

'What do you mean, is that all?'

Anita paused and took a deep breath. Laurence hadn't mentioned the photos. She clung on to that.

'I was in The Hesperia, though, towards the end, not in your apartment,' she said.

'Really? What do you mean?'

283

'It's totally no business of yours but I'll tell you anyway. I moved in with a guy called Connor. Obviously it was a mistake. Which I regret. He wasn't the most . . .' She tailed off.

Laurence shuddered.

'I couldn't drive,' she said. 'I started having panic attacks. Connor helped me out. We drove around Dobrich together.'

'So you moved in with him. As one does . . .'

'Larry. There's no point in looking at me like that.'

'Mossy . . .'

'Please, Larry. It was a mistake. I've said so. You won't understand because you're a man, but sometimes, when someone is kind to you and you feel obliged to him, you sort of get in a position where . . .'

'Isn't thank you sufficient? I would have thought a bottle of Johnny Walker.'

16

The bar in Clerkenwell had filled up. After-work conversation, raucous and hearty, was loudest around the bar. The crowd seemed miles away, as though at the end of a field; the talking and laughing as innocent as school playtime. A group of women gathered at the end of the table where Anita and Laurence were sitting. They shed their outdoor clothes. The coats and jackets were now strewn on the benches in untidy piles. The women leant forward towards each other, all girls together, sharing joint ownership of tight tops and cleavage. They chinked glasses.

With the rising noise levels, Anita had to strain to hear Laurence.

'And now, the holiday's permanent,' he said. 'That's the idea, anyway. They don't want a lot; nowhere massive, a small apartment where they can have a few drinks on the terrace. A pool for the summer. Another buy-to-let to finance the project. They're going to The Hesperia next month to get the feel of it – though they'll probably end up buying in Spain or Portugal. My father speaks a

bit of Spanish. He had business connections in Argentina.'
Laurence leant forward. 'Have another nut, Mossy. Take
a handful.'

His pensiveness had passed, replaced by a kind of
confidence that assumed rightful possession. She felt
uneasy. After his last trip to the bar, he had chosen to
sit close beside her again.

Anita was wearing one of her less successful outfits
– not so much flung together as fastened on, held in
place by thinness and a whisper and topped by a chunky
cardigan with leather-covered buttons. Although the bar
had warmed up, she was reluctant to discard her top
layer. Laurence had several times glanced down at the
clothes. His eyes lingered on her. She regretted the story
about Connor.

'Perpetual holiday. It sounds all right,' Anita said,
sipping her third glass of Argentinian red.

'Could be. Could be perfect. My mother's not totally
onside.'

'I'm sorry?' she said.

'"Won't it be a tie, always going to the same place?
Supposing cheap flights come to an end?"' Laurence put
on a soprano voice that struck Anita as hardly credible.

'Some people say we shouldn't be flying at all,' she
said.

'Never stops them though, does it? Self-righteous twats.

The planes are going to fly, whether I'm on them or not,' Laurence said.

'The righteous ones drink hot Bovril from a thermos on the front at Frinton, as flights from Stansted pass overhead between the clouds,' Anita said.

'Bovril. It's a long time since I heard that mentioned.' He glanced at her. 'Did you and Connor drink it, of an evening?'

'No.'

'I thought, maybe, an additional surprise revelation was in the offing; a little circumstantial detail.' Laurence picked up his glass and downed it. 'Another, Mossy?'

'No, thanks, Larry. I ought to be getting home.'

'Remind me where home is. Fulham?'

He enjoyed his moment of malice. It endured in the form of a half-smile when they got on to talking about where they lived. Swiss Cottage and World's End, Chelsea. Laurence knew Anita's street. He had never been down it but he had seen it from the Embankment and Gunter Grove. He had often got stuck in traffic.

From there, he returned to property prices. Anita longed to be home. She avoided the look in Laurence's eye and stopped listening.

'My sister, who's a tad pinko, blamed British Waterways. But why shouldn't they release capital if it suits them? The man put up a fight, getting local people to sign a petition.

He tried to raise the money to buy the place himself, but the developers won in the end. They outbid him.'

The women at the end of the table were whooping with laughter. Anita missed chunks of what Laurence was saying.

'Where are we talking about, Larry? I didn't know you had a sister. I've lost track.'

'Alison. You must meet her. I think you'd get on. She and her husband live in the 'burbs. Cheshunt in Hertfordshire. Not far from the River Lea. They've got rather a nice place; a Victorian villa.'

It took a second to register what Laurence had said. There was so much noise. She felt her body flood with some unpleasant cold substance.

Laurence put his hand over hers. 'I know, Mossy,' he said with meaning.

Her fear returned; it hit her with an upward thrust in the solar plexus. As she took the impact, she caught her breath.

'What do you know?' she asked.

'I saw the story in Alison's local rag – with a picture of the lock-keeper's cottage. I love local papers, don't you? There's something so naïve about them. It's the mix, I think.' He kept his eye on her as he spoke.

She was silent. 'So, what has happened?' she asked quietly, feeling her way.

'The usual planning delays, I suspect. Additions will follow; a double garage, a dinky conservatory.'

'No. Your website. Have there been complaints? Have you withdrawn it?'

He turned to her. The headmaster's expression again – his face very close. It was as if, a few inches away, a giant face were being pieced together on a makeshift hoarding. A fleshy slice of nose, a gooseberry eye. 'Why did you do it, Mossy?'

'Just tell me what's happened. Please.'

The blurred mouth was clamped shut.

'Larry?'

He hesitated. 'I didn't go through with the project. Partly the lack of photographic material.' His eyes accused, then blinked. 'Partly the turbulence in the financial markets.'

She stared at him.

'I kept trying to see you,' he said. 'I wanted to discuss this weeks ago. We could have cleared it up. And progressed to . . .'

She closed her eyes, expecting relief, but none came. Instead, she felt old and semi-paralysed.

'Why, Mossy?'

She opened her eyes. His face was still there, a little further away now – in focus – and the hand, which in her numbness she had ceased to feel, had transferred to her thigh.

'Do you know, I can't be bothered to go into it all?'

He smiled. 'Tell me some other time. Let's forget it now. We'll go and have dinner at Bruno's. Or would you like another drink first?'

He gave her thigh a squeeze. She saw he was pleased with himself, having fed his gleaned information by drip method. He held the power. He could afford to be magnanimous. She would have to make excuses every step of the way. If not dinner, then sharing a taxi. He would be solicitous and take her all the way home, although it was the wrong direction. Then he would expect to come in. He would, perhaps, have banked on that even without the story of Connor. Tiredness overcame her.

'No, I must get back, Larry. Truly. We'll have dinner together soon, I promise.'

She bent down to pick up her coat which had slithered off the bench.

The outdoor crowd had dispersed. Two smokers remained. They were nothing to do with one another. They stood under different parts of the awning, like bookends. She and Laurence put up their umbrellas; his – capacious and black with a polished wooden handle and brass rivet – lapped over hers. She adjusted her grip and attempted

290

to keep her own space in the rain. A stray spoke stuck out at an angle. Laurence insisted, when she refused a taxi, on walking her to Farringdon Station.

Under the street lights, the pavements glistened greasily. As they walked along, the conversation was like pass the parcel with the music stopping at Laurence. He undid the wrapping and out fell disparate items. Anita's own contributions seemed small islands of nonsense.

Traffic swooshed along Clerkenwell Road. Farringdon Lane, when they reached it, was dug up. Outside the station was a vast hole, contained within temporary barriers. A crane stretched up towards the sky, linking everlasting construction with deep excavation. They entered the station and said goodbye at the ticket barrier. She must, for once, have sounded firm. He kissed her lightly on the lips.

Waiting on the platform, she tried to forget Laurence and the glint in his eye, as blatant as a televised close-up of Count Almaviva. She hadn't disavowed her earlier story about Connor – or disowned him. It would have been wrong to mock the faraway man who, in a parallel reality, had scored without knowing it. Fran would get to hear the story. She would fill Laurence in on the dyed hair. She and Laurence would look at each other in mock astonishment.

On balance, she was grateful to Connor for stopping

the car from smashing into the glass doors of The Hesperia, though she suspected he had partly caused the situation. The almighty bang, as his fist came down on the console, was a variation on the therapeutic slap to bring someone hysterical to her senses. Her panic had panicked him – and maybe all such thwacks stem from a sudden, blind intolerance towards the weak.

It puzzled Anita that she responded in the same intemperate way to the trivial and to the serious. Panic failed to distinguish between the real and the imagined, the past or the present. One day, perhaps, humans would evolve into beings whose fine gradations of reasoning – assuming they still had any – were mirrored in the body.

The train was crowded and the carriage she stepped into full of young women out on a hen night. Since they were dressed identically in short, tight, black dresses, draped with pink feather boas, Anita would have known what they were celebrating even without the banner inscribed *Michelle's Hen Party*, which two of them were carrying. It hung loosely between them and tautened with the swaying of the carriage. Both girls clung, one-handed, to the safety rails, unstable on stiletto heels.

The other passengers, half asphyxiated by wafts of

perfume, ignored them. Eyes down, iPods on, they kept to themselves. Hidden in darkness, under the hood of a buggy, a baby slept. The girls bumped together, singing in fractured unison. The train continued westwards round the Circle Line.

At Mansion House, through the din, Anita caught the words of an amplified announcement. The woman speaking sounded composed, as if she could tolerate anything.

'The next station is closed. Passengers should exit here and continue their journey at street level.'

The woman's calm was exemplary. Had she thought, as she recorded the message, of the scenes she would speak over?

Street level. Although Anita's destination was many stops away, she was reassured by the words. The train whooshed out of the tunnel. She could, if she wished, stand up, steer past Michelle in her tiara, and wait for the doors to open.